Lady
A Regency Mystery

Death, Where Is Thy Sting?

Hilary Gilman

Pleasant Street Publications
Cover Design by Lee Wright, Halo Studios London
www.halostudios.co.uk

By the same author

Historical Romance

Moonlight Masquerade
Mysterious Masquerade
Merry Masquerade
Magical Masquerade
Midsummer Masquerade
Milady's Masquerade

Dangerous Escapade
(first published as Dangerous Masquerade)

Gamble with Hearts
The Cautious Heart
Her Foolish Heart
A Match of Hearts
The Captured Heart
Hearts Beguiled

Fantasy
Tides of Fire Book I: The Rebellion
The Golden Queen: Tides of Fire Book II
(as Hilary Lester)

Contents

Prologue: Poor Isabella

The three Misses Rose were all remarkably handsome. Mama had been a great beauty in her day, though sadly lacking in fortune, and it had quite astonished the Ton when she threw away her chances of making a good match to elope with an improvident, though handsome, younger son.

Sadly, Mama had succumbed to a particularly bad bout of influenza when her youngest girl was but five years old; and Papa, not inconsolable, had been little seen in the crumbling ancestral home in Nottinghamshire during the following ten years. However, one bitterly cold morning in February, some eight months after Wellington's great victory at Waterloo, the eldest Miss Rose received a letter from her erratic parent.

It was brought to her as the girls were sitting at breakfast, clustered as close as possible in front of an inadequate fire. The table was presided over by Miss Proudie, their erstwhile governess, true friend and current chaperone.

'What does your Papa have to say?' she presently asked in her rather abrupt accents. 'Not good news, I'll be bound.'

Isabella Rose carefully laid down the letter. She was rather white and, though she attempted to smile, her lip trembled. 'No, not good news, dear.'

Miss Marianne Rose jumped from her seat and put her arms around her sister's shoulders. 'Bella, what is it?'

Isabella took a deep breath and said with an effort, 'Prepare yourself for a shock, my love. Papa writes to say that he—he—' Unable to continue, she handed the letter to Miss Proudie and buried her face in her hands.

Miss Proudie soon made herself mistress of the contents. In a voice almost totally devoid of emotion, she said, 'My dears, you will have to make your preparations to leave Thistledown Grange. The house has been sold, and your father wishes you to join him in London.'

'Leave Thistledown?' Marianne looked rather relieved. 'Well, that is not so terrible, is it? I mean, this winter has almost killed us.'

'That is not quite all. Your papa has received an offer for Isabella's hand in marriage, which, he writes, he has accepted on her behalf.'

'How exciting! Who is it?'

'My dear Marianne, can you not see how overset your sister is? Do you imagine this is a cause for rejoicing?'

Marianne's face fell. 'I'm sorry, I didn't think.'

'Is it someone horrid?' demanded Miss Abigail with all the forthrightness of her fifteen years.

'It is—the Earl of Guisborough,' said Isabella in tragic accents.

'Oh? Is there something wrong with him? I mean, it must be a good thing to be a—an—earl-ess.'

'A countess, silly!' scolded Miss Marianne.

'Well, but still— Is he very much in love with you, Bella? Where did you meet him?'

Isabella bit her lip. 'I have met him only once, at the assembly in Lincoln. He—he asked me to stand up with him.'

'He must have fallen in love with you at first sight!'

Isabella tried to smile. 'I do not know. He looked at me so strangely—so—fixedly—he quite frightened me.'

'Well, but why else should he have offered for you, Bella? You don't have any fortune or connections or anything.'

Miss Proudie interposed, 'I doubt if there is another young lady of good birth in the country whose father would consider his offer for a moment. Your Papa must be out of his—but I should not speak so of him to you.'

Marianne shrugged. 'We have no illusions about Papa, I assure you, Ma'am. But, why is the Earl so ineligible?'

'Because, my dear Marianne, it is universally believed that he murdered his first wife.'

Marianne stared. 'What happened to her?'

'She was found at dawn on the terrace at Coningsby Park clad only in her nightgown. She had fallen from the battlements above. And her neck was broken.'

One: Lady Cavendish Receives a Letter

Lady Cavendish had been married for two years, and she was, by this time, accustomed to a circumstance that had bewildered her during her first few months as a bride. This was that, after a rapturous night passed in the arms of her handsome, ardent, adoring husband, the following morning, he became grumpy, taciturn and, when forced to speak, would bark at her. This effect—one had to be just—only persisted until his third cup of coffee and so did not, she had decided, constitute a sufficient reason to dissolve an otherwise blissfully happy union.

While Sir Dominic perused the morning paper, she sipped her own coffee and opened her correspondence, carefully removing the seals with her butter knife, as her eight-year-old nephew, Bobby, more properly titled 'Lord Fanshawe,' was making a collection.

'Oh! Good Gracious!'

This exclamation, uttered in tones of distress, was enough to make Dominic put down his newspaper. 'What is it?'

'This letter!'

'Yes, I'd gathered that. Don't dither, Sweetheart. What is in it?'

'It's from Miss Proudie.'

Dominic yawned. 'What does the old trout have to say?'

'Isabella Rose is married!'

'Is she? I wish her very happy. Could I have another cup of coffee?'

'No—I mean—yes you can have another cup of coffee—but, no, you do not understand. She has married the Earl of Guisborough!'

'Well?'

'Don't be stupid, Dominic. You know what they call him.'

'The Prince of Darkness,' he uttered in a thrilling whisper, rolling his eyes. 'Don't be a silly goose. There's nothing wrong with Guisborough.'

'How do you know?'

'He's very sound on the Emancipation Question.'

'He looks like Richard the Third,' said Cecily with an eloquent shudder.

'You mean, he looks like Edmund Kean *playing* Richard the Third. Hardly his fault.'

'Well, Miss Proudie is desperately worried. She says Isabella is very unwell—'

'I suppose she thinks Guisborough is poisoning her?'

'Well, yes—she does.'

'Why on earth should he marry the girl just to do away with her? It's not as though she were an heiress, and, even if she were, he's one of the wealthiest men in England.' He saw that Cecily looked really distressed and stretched out his hand to her across the breakfast plates. 'I'm sorry, Sweetheart. What else does she say?'

'She wants us to investigate. Because we were so successful in solving the murder at Heron Lodge.'[1]

He gave a shout of laughter. 'We certainly were brilliant there! I cleverly deduced the murderer's identity the instant I saw him with his hands about your throat.'

She dimpled at him. 'That is true. We were all wrong about him. But no one else even thought that it had been a murder at all.'

'Nurse did.'

'Nurse could help us again.'

'Come here,' he said, pulling her out of her seat and establishing her upon his knee with his arms about her waist. 'Now, do you really want to go to Lincolnshire and investigate?'

She picked up a napkin, wiped a little egg from the corner of his mouth, and kissed him. 'Yes, I do. I was very fond of Isabella Rose at school and, besides, it is far too long since we visited Kate and Lion and—and—all our friends in Alford.'

---

[1] The Captured Heart

'I knew it! This is just an excuse to be with your lover!'

'Dominic! How can you? Peter is not, and has never been, my lover.'

'He wanted to be.'

'He wanted to marry me. That is not the same thing at all.'

'Isn't it?' he said with meaning and cupped her head with his hand, drawing her in for a kiss. 'Husbands can be lovers, can't they, my darling?'

She blushed and answered rather breathlessly, 'Not at nine o'clock in the morning.'

'Why not? Have you somewhere you need to be?'

'No.'

'You do now.'

****

Cecily pulled herself up against the pillows, stretched, and sighed. Being a married lady certainly was the nicest thing. But she must get up—again—and tidy herself. The servants were far too discreet to enter the room until their master had left for the day, but the housemaid would certainly be cross if her work were to be delayed any further.

She glanced around the room, thinking how charming the new furniture and draperies looked. She was very happy with the narrow little white house Dominic had purchased for her in Albemarle Street. It was a convenient distance from Whitehall, where he had taken a position in a department so shadowy that very few people even knew it existed; and it was equally favourable for her in its proximity to all the delights of Bond Street, Hatchard's, and Hyde Park.

She had new furnished it from top to bottom in the first style of elegance. She had filled it with flowers, books, music boxes, and friends. In it, she supervised her servants, consulted with her cook and, exquisitely gowned, welcomed her handsome husband home every evening to a perfect dinner.

But that morning, as the door slammed behind Dominic

and she was faced with another day of unqualified pleasure, she sighed. Something was missing, and she knew very well what that 'something' was. She had been married for two years and, although Mama said that there was nothing unusual in her situation, and there was no occasion to be concerned, she did long for a baby to make her happiness quite perfect. However, darling Dominic had been so very ardent that morning—perhaps—?

Returning to the breakfast parlour, Cecily picked up Miss Proudie's letter and read it though again with more attention. Her former teacher really seemed most uncharacteristically agitated.

It began conventionally enough: *My dear Lady Cavendish, I beg you will forgive me for writing to you upon this occasion, which I fear you may consider an impertinence. You will remember that, upon my retirement from Miss Johnson's Academy, where I had the honour to be your teacher, I took a private position in the house of Mr Rose in Nottinghamshire. Isabella Rose was, of course, a fellow pupil of yours at the Academy, although a few years lower, but I know you will remember her.*

Cecily smiled and laid down the letter. How could anyone forget Isabella Rose? If ever a girl could be described as a flower of England, Isabella was that girl—such golden hair, such blue eyes, such a complexion, and a disposition as sweet as her smile. She picked up the letter once more.

You may, perhaps, be aware that Isabella is lately married to the Earl of Guisborough. I need hardly tell you how I viewed the prospect of this marriage, how strongly I advised against it, but to no avail. Isabella was sold—I can call it nothing else—by her father and sacrificed herself for his advantage and that of her sisters.

From this point, the letter grew increasingly melodramatic. From almost the first moment of her arrival at Coningsby Park, Isabella had been struck with a wasting sickness. She was under the constant attendance of a doctor.

But nothing could be done and, most frightening of all, she had begun to walk at night, just like her predecessor, and had been found, in her nightgown, upon the highest point of the battlements. Her eyes had been open, but her consciousness had been in complete suspension.

In another incident, Isabella had been found after midnight outside the tiny chapel in the grounds of Coningsby Park. She was fully awake but claimed she had followed the ghost of Guisborough's first wife to the tomb where she lay. When her husband approached to soothe her, she showed extreme terror and fainted. The medical man brought down from London took a grave view and talked of her being locked up for her own protection.

Cecily wiped a tear from her cheek as she laid down the missive. To think of lovely, delicate Isabella in such a situation! It was horrible. 'Something must be done!' she vowed, with a determined jut of her pretty chin that her husband would have recognised. 'Isabella is as sane as I am.'

In proof of her own sanity, she spent the rest of the day muttering to herself as she marshalled the arguments she would use to coax Dominic into doing as she wished. A fashionable matron in Gunter's was startled to be told that 'a woman's life may depend upon it!' and a costermonger took it in extremely bad part when he was apostrophised as a 'selfish, self-centred idiot.'

Too experienced a wife to attack her husband before he had eaten his dinner, she had ordered her cook to prepare Dominic's favourite dishes. Since his tastes ran very much to roast game, meat pies, and beefsteaks, this did not tax Cook's culinary skills to any great extent. But, as that lady said, she liked to see a gentleman eat hearty, and at least the platters were never sent back to the kitchen untouched.

Having catered for her husband's inner man, Cecily prepared her attack on another front, namely, his manly weakness in the face of woman's wiles. Fortunately, a new gown had been sent home that very day, and it was one she was sure Dominic would approve, being a diaphanous cloud of mauve voile, worn over a satin slip that did nothing to disguise her shape beneath. She had already determined to send back the slip—which was really too abbreviated for decency—and she would never have dared to go out in it; but she would wear it this once in a just cause.

She was attired in this creation and reclining languorously on a pale-green striped, brocade sofa when she heard the front door open to admit Dominic who came tempestuously into the room, calling, 'Pack your bags, my darling—we're off to Lincolnshire at dawn!' He stopped short at the alluring beauty that met his eyes, swooped down, picked her up in his arms, and kissed her.

Cecily was pleased with the effect of her gown but rather cross that all her careful plans had proved needless. When she was able to speak, she said, straightening her skirts, 'What made you change your mind, Dominic? You didn't seem at all inclined to rescue poor Isabella this morning.'

'Isabella? Oh, it has nothing to do with her. No—Raoul and Abby are back in Alford!'

'Oh? Well, that is lovely, of course, but why do we have to dash down to see them like this?'

'Orders, Cecily, orders. The Minister wants me to recruit Raoul. After all, the poor fellow must be bored to death now Boney has been finally defeated.'

'But you know Raoul would never agree to act in any way against France, even if his beloved emperor is in exile. He is a patriot.'

'Of course, he is. But he is also a superb sea-captain and knows the waters around Europe and Africa like the back of his hand. We want him to help stamp out the slave trade on the coast of West Africa. If he really believes in *liberté, égalité, fraternité*, this is his chance to prove it.'

'Is *that* what your department does? I never knew.'

'We're co-ordinating operations, among other things that I can't possibly discuss with you.'

'Yes, I know—you swore an oath—you have told me so about a hundred times.'

'I swore an oath to you, too, if you remember. To love and to cherish you. I take it you wouldn't want to be married to a man who would break his word? If you break one oath—why not them all?'

'As if you would!' She stood on tiptoe to kiss his cheek just as the door opened and her butler announced that dinner was served.

As she shook out her napkin and laid it upon her lap, Cecily said, 'Since we are going to be in Alford, in any event, could we not kill two birds with one stone and just look into this case? I absolutely refuse to believe that my poor little friend is going mad, but the only other explanation seems to be that she is being haunted by Guisborough's first wife. And—apart from the fact that I don't believe in ghosts—that doesn't explain how the first Lady Guisborough died. Unless he murdered her, and you said you don't believe that.'

Dominic looked up from the pheasant he was carving. 'I can see you are not going to talk about anything else all through dinner, so you might as well tell me all about it straightaway.'

By the time Cecily had finished her tale, the pheasant had been cleared away and a veal chop, swimming in a creamy mushroom sauce, had replaced it. However, while Dominic had been eating he had paid attention to her story and, when she ceased to speak, he said, 'Obviously, a drug of some kind. It is the only explanation.'

'Yes, I thought that too. But who is feeding it to her—and why?'

'I cannot tell you who, but I am pretty sure I know why.'

'Well?'

'To destroy Guisborough.'

'Guisborough? But it is Isabella—'

'Yes, it is Isabella who is being harmed, but I'll wager that it is Guisborough who is the real target.'

17

'Why would you say that?' Cecily was inclined to be annoyed by this lofty disregard for Isabella's peril.

'Think it out, darling. The attacks, if they are indeed attacks, commenced the moment the girl arrived at the Park. No one there could have anything against Isabella—as Isabella. It is Lady Guisborough that is the intended victim, not Isabella Rose.'

'Oh! And, of course, the first Lady Guisborough died the same way—I mean—not that poor Isabella is—you know what I mean.'

He laughed. 'Strangely enough I do. And it strengthens my point. Someone is determined that Guisborough shall not be a happily married man.'

'It is a sneaking, cowardly way to strike at a man— through his wife!'

He smiled at her across the covers and reached out a hand. 'Sweetheart, didn't our adventures at Heron Lodge serve to convince you that murderers are, always, sneaking and cowardly?'

'True,' she nodded, reflecting on the only murderer with whom, as far as she was aware, she had been acquainted. She tucked her hand in his and gave a little sigh. 'It will be very nice to see Raoul and Abby again. She did not mention that they were coming home in her last letter.'

'No, I fancy the Squire is unwell.'

'Nothing serious, I hope?'

'I cannot tell. I think not.'

Cecily looked down and traced a pattern upon the tablecloth with one finger. 'It will be lovely to see their baby. He must be nearly two years old.'

'Not very tactful, Cecily. They have only been married a couple of months longer than us.'

'He came early!'

'What? Six months early?'

Cecily giggled. 'But Raoul said that Abby should be as sacred as the Holy Mother to him until they were married.'

'What Raoul says, and what Raoul does, are often two different things. But, in this case, I imagine that it was Abby who got tired of waiting. She was always an impatient girl.'

'Well, you should know.'

Cecily was very fond of all Dominic's childhood friends, but occasionally she could not prevent a little spurt of jealousy. They were all so close, still, and had so much shared past. It was nicer here in London where she could have Dominic all to herself. Then she was ashamed of herself. Abby had always been kindness itself, and no one could have better friends than Lion and Kate Leonard.

'Well, I'm sure I do not blame her, if it were so,' she said. 'They had hardly landed in France when Raoul had to go off and join the army. She might never have seen him again. At least she would have had—memories.'

'Something a little more substantial than a memory,' was his only comment.

'Sometimes I think you don't have an ounce of romance in your soul.'

'Romance is all very well,' he said, looking at her for once without a smile in his eyes. 'But to be married to the woman you love means far more than that. It is to have the strength of two to face every trouble, every danger that life can throw at you.' His unwonted seriousness was dissolved in a grin. 'And, if you are going to insist on investigating every mystery that comes your way, we shall have plenty of both to occupy us.'

Two: Consultation in the Vicarage Garden

'I consider that it is of the first importance to introduce Nurse into the Park,' announced Kate Leonard as she, Dominic, Cecily, and Miss Proudie were gathered in the charming, untidy Vicarage garden watching the children at play. Bobby, who now lived with the Leonards, was, as usual, hand-in-hand with Pricilla, a little heartbreaker of six years, while the elder children were variously engaged in cricket, hide-and-seek or, in the case of the eldest boy, with a book.

'There is no one I would trust to protect Lady Guisborough more than I would Nurse,' agreed Dominic.

'Very true,' nodded Cecily. 'I feel just the same. But how is it to be done? I expect Lord Guisborough has servants of his own that he regards just as highly as we do Nurse.'

'There will not be the smallest difficulty,' answered Miss Proudie in her clipped, decisive way. 'The servants at the Park are in mortal terror of approaching the poor child, especially at night.'

'But why?'

'For fear that the ghost of the first Lady Guisborough should appear.' Miss Proudie looked down her nose in disapproval. 'Though why they should fear the manifestation of a lady who was, as far as one can ascertain, a sweet and gentle mistress, adored by the household, I cannot tell. Why should she be thought to be malevolent in death when beneficent in life?'

Cecily shuddered. 'Well, I should not like to meet a ghost, however charming someone was before they died!'

'I thought you didn't believe in ghosts,' remarked her husband, who was stretched comfortably upon the turf at her feet, with the Vicarage cat snoozing upon his chest.

'I don't. All I am saying is that—if there are such things— I should prefer not to meet one.'

'I concur with Lady Cavendish,' said Lion Leonard, who had appeared in the garden in time to hear this exchange. 'I don't believe in ghosts, either, at three o'clock on a sunny afternoon. I cannot answer for my courage at midnight in Coningsby Park, however.'

'Here's a thought,' said Dominic, sitting up suddenly so that the cat, sliding down his chest, dug in her claws and regarded him through baleful, half-closed eyes. 'Could you not perform an exorcism or something, old fellow?'

Lion looked doubtful. 'I suppose I could, although I do not know what the Bishop would say.'

'I fail to see what good an exorcism might be supposed to be against a flesh-and-blood poisoner,' said Miss Proudie, rather impatiently.

'My dear Ma'am, he or she has, until now, had things all his—or her—own way. We must force him—or her—'

'For goodness sake, Dominic! Just say "the murderer" or something,' begged his wife.

'No one has been murdered yet,' he objected.

'What about the first Lady Guisborough?'

'We do not know that. Her death, and the manner of it, might simply have given someone ideas. In any event, it will put a spoke in his—or—' He caught his wife's eye and finished, hastily, '—the murderer's wheel.'

'If you think it would help, I'll ask the Bish for his permission. He's a cheery old cove and might well think it a great lark.'

'We are getting off the point,' interrupted Cecily, firmly. 'Once Nurse is installed, she can watch over everything Isabella eats or drinks; but it does not help us discover who he—or she—now I'm doing it!—is.'

Kate rummaged in her reticule and pulled out a little memorandum book and a pencil. 'Let us make a list of those close enough to Lady Guisborough to administer the drug. Then we can see where we are.'

'Oh, excellent, Kate!' said Dominic, reaching for her hand and kissing it. 'You are quite right. We must be practical.'

'You do not know what the word means, Dom,' she told him, laughing. She licked the tip of her pencil and held it poised over the page. 'Now, who is the most likely culprit?'

'Lord Guisborough, of course,' said Cecily.

'Why? Why should he try to poison the girl whom he just married and, presumably, is in love with?' demanded Dominic reasonably.

'No, Dom, she is right,' Kate admonished him. 'We are discussing opportunity. People commit crimes for all manner of reasons that seem ridiculous to normal people. Guisborough might just enjoy murdering his wives. The question is, does he have the opportunity?'

'Well, of course. He is the only one of the household who may approach his wife at any hour, day or night and insist on being alone with her.'

'Except that he does not,' interposed Miss Proudie, in a dry tone.

'I beg your pardon?'

'The Earl of Guisborough does not visit his wife's bedchamber, either by day or night.'

'What—never?'

'Never since—well—just at first, you know.'

'How very odd,' commented Cecily.

'Not at all. If his wife is unwell, it shows a very commendable restraint,' protested Dominic.

'I did not mean that!' She blushed and said in a quieter tone, 'I mean, if she is unwell, you would think her husband would be concerned and—and—wish to see how she goes on.'

'Apparently not.' Kate wrote 'The Earl of Guisborough' and placed a large number one next to it. 'Who else?'

'Are we including the servants?' asked Dominic.

'Of course. One of them might be in the murderer's employ.'

'Well, then, her abigail is an obvious possibility. Unless she has known her since she were a baby or some such. Has she, Miss Proudie?'

'No. She has only recently joined the staff at the Park.'

'And who engaged her?'

'Lord Guisborough.'

'What do you think of her, Ma'am?' asked Dominic. 'Do you like her?'

'She is a sly one—being French, you know, but I do not think she is wicked.'

'Nevertheless, she has opportunity,' said Kate. 'What is her name?'

'Marie-Claire Martin.'

'Number two,' wrote Kate. 'What about the cook? If anyone can put poison in Isabella's food, she can.'

Miss Proudie shook her head. 'The Earl has a chef, not a cook. He paid him a small fortune to leave London and work for him. I do not think the man has any interest in murder or anything else outside his own domain.'

'We can discuss his reasons later. He has opportunity,' Kate reminded her.

'But how could he ensure that Isabella ate the poisoned food and not the Earl? Surely, the dishes are placed on the table and everyone served from the same platters,' said Cecily. 'Is that not so, Miss Proudie?'

'The poor child is rarely well enough to dine with his Lordship now. It would be easy enough for anyone in the house to tamper with her tray.'

'We do not seem to be getting on at all,' complained Cecily.

'Very well,' said Kate. 'We will agree that all the inhabitants of the Park have opportunity. What about outside the Park? Are there any regular visitors?'

'Well, there is the doctor, of course.'

'Not dear Doctor Carter!' cried Cecily. 'I absolutely refuse to believe—'

Kate laughed. 'Doctor Carter is not the only doctor in Lincolnshire, you know, Cecily. Who is attending her, Miss Proudie?'

'Doctor Stewart. A very distinguished man. Studied in Edinburgh and Paris.'

'I wonder what induced him to settle in Coningsby.'

'I believe he and the Earl were at Eton together.'

'Ah—an accomplice!'

'Cecily!'

She had the grace to look a little guilty. 'Well, he could be,' she muttered.

'Do not forget Mr Tweedie, the vicar of Saint Martin's,' Lion reminded his wife. 'He dines at the Park and plays chess with Guisborough, quite frequently.'

'Really, Lion. Take this seriously,' scolded his wife.

'Why not? Men of the cloth have gone off their heads before now,' he said, unrepentant.

'Is there anyone else?' asked Kate, refusing this gambit. 'There must be.'

'There is the apothecary, Mr Newman, and his son who is learning the trade. Both very respectable, I have no doubt.'

'Poisoning customers is bad for business,' said Dominic irrepressibly.

'And then there is—me,' interposed Miss Proudie.

There was a general shout of disapprobation, but she held up her hand for silence. 'You cannot acquit me. I am staying at the Park. I am in and out of Isabella's chamber at all hours—which is why I know that her husband is not—and old-maid school teachers are just as likely to "go off their heads" as churchmen, I assure you.'

Cecily stood and stepped across the lawn to where Miss Proudie sat, stiff and upright upon a wrought-iron garden chair. 'I should as soon suspect my own dear Mama as you, Ma'am,' she said, and stooped to kiss the lady's cheek. 'So let us have no more such nonsense.'

Miss Proudie's lips quivered, and a hint of moisture appeared in her eyes. 'Thank you, my dear.'

Dominic, who had been watching his wife with a softened face, said in the tone of one getting back to business, 'There is one person whose opinion might be of the greatest value to us.'

Kate looked up from her memorandum. 'Who is that, Dom?'

'Isabella herself. Tell me, Ma'am, what does she believe is happening to her? Has she confided in you?'

Miss Proudie, having wiped away a slight trickle of moisture, shook her head. 'The dear child will only say that she is sure she will soon be well. Her loyalty to her husband is praiseworthy but, I think, misguided. Before she married him, she told me that he frightened her.'

'Do you think she might talk to me?' asked Cecily. 'I mean, as we are old friends and both quite newly married, she might perhaps not be—on her guard—so to speak.'

'She might. She speaks of you always with great affection.'

'Then Dominic shall drive me over tomorrow and, while I am closeted with Isabella, he may quiz her husband.'

'And how am I supposed to do that?'

She gave him a scornful look. 'With your extensive experience of spies and smugglers and slave-traders, I think you are probably more than a match for an English nobleman, even if he is a murderous maniac.'

'Spy and smuggler I admit. *C'est vrai,*' came a merry voice in her ear. 'But slaver? *Non et non et non*!'

She looked up to find Raoul de Saint Michel bending over her chair. 'Raoul! I did not know you were here!'

He swiftly kissed her lips, with one laughing eye upon her husband. 'You permit, *mon ami*?'

'Aye, but that's enough,' said Dominic, rising to his feet and advancing with his hand held out. Raoul, however, ignored the hand and instead seized his friend in a fond embrace, kissing him on each cheek. Dominic, feeling himself unable to return the gesture, contented himself with giving his old enemy a few hearty slaps on the back.

'Where's Abby?'

'With the poor papa at Chertsey House. But I am charged with many messages of love and to bring you both to her as soon as may be. Will you dine with us tomorrow?'

'Are you sure?' said Cecily, a little anxiously. 'Is not the household in disarray with the master so ill?'

'It was, but my Abby has set all to rights in a trice. That woman is *une merveille, un ange.* I have no words!'

'I would never have guessed it,' remarked Dominic. 'Aye, we'll dine with you. I wanted a word with you.'

'A word with me?' Saint Michel looked a little wary. 'I am enchanted, my dear friend, naturally.'

Dominic laughed. 'I am not dragging up the past. You kept your word and stayed out of British affairs—as far as I know.'

'*Naturellement*! I am a man of honour!'

'I hope we are both that. In any event, it is your future I want to discuss with you, not your past.'

Raoul's expression changed. The mask of levity was banished, and he said in a tired voice, 'What future? My Emperor in exile, my chateau in ruins, my lands laid waste, and no money to set things to rights. It is a pretty picture, *hein*?'

'How if I could show you a way to make your fortune— would you be interested?'

Raoul looked at him sharply. 'It is not to bring any harm to my country?'

'I would not ask such a thing of you.'

'Then of course, I am very interested, indeed.'

They were interrupted by the tempestuous arrival of my Lord Fanshawe who had dropped Pricilla's hand at the sight of the Marquis and now ran straight at him, calling, 'Captain Raoul! Captain Raoul!'

Saint Michel received him in a comprehensive embrace and then held him a little away from him. '*Mon petit ami*, let me look at you. But how you have grown!'

'Yes, I know. I am eight now, and I am ten inches taller than I was when you went away.'

'But you are a young giant!'

'Indeed,' said Kate fondly, 'He eats us out of house and home.'

'And remember, you promised that, when I was big, you would let me sail with you as your cabin boy.'

The Marquis sighed. 'But, *mon cher*, I no longer have a ship to sail; and, even if I did, you are a Lord and I a Marquis, and we may no longer go adventuring together.'

'But you promised!'

'Alas, I am desolate—but *noblesse oblige, Monseigneur. Noblesse oblige.*'

For a moment, Bobby looked mutinous, but, then, Pricilla appeared at his side and slipped a hand in his. 'You can't go away with that man with the funny voice,' she said in a scolding accent. 'You have to stay here and take care of me.'

Saint Michel laughed. 'Another and more enchanting obligation for you. Most certainly you must guard *Mademoiselle*, or some impudent fellow may steal her from you.'

'I should like to see him try,' rejoined Bobby, making them all laugh.

Kate said, in an under-voice to Cecily, 'My poor little Pricilla. She adores him but, in another year or so, he will scorn to be seen in her company, or he will tease and terrify her. He is just like Dom.'

'Perhaps. But when they are both older, it would be charming—'

'What are you two whispering about?' demanded Dominic.

'We are settling the children's future,' Kate told him with a shamefaced little laugh. 'Foolish, I know.'

'Very foolish. You and I vowed to marry each other once, I remember. And now look at us.'

At that moment, Cecily rose and called her husband to order. 'If we are to be at your grandmother's house by dinnertime, we must leave now.' She lightly embraced her hostess and smiled upon the gentlemen. 'I hate to leave you all.'

'How do you agree with the dowager?' asked Kate as she walked with them back into the house.

Cecily dropped her voice. 'She's a dragon!'

'I know. I was always scared to death of her.'

'You never know what she will say to put one to the blush. When we visited her after our wedding, she told me that there was more to marriage than four bare legs in a bed. Can you imagine?'

'Women know that—it's the men who need to be told,' said Kate, laughing.

'What do we need to be told?' said Dominic, coming up behind them, having stayed behind for a private word with Saint Michel.

'How to treat your wives.'

'Oh, there is no mystery about that,' said Dominic outrageously. '*A woman, a dog, and a walnut tree, the more you beat them the better they be!*'

'Dom!'

'Don't be concerned, Kate,' said Cecily kindly. 'If there is any beating to be done—I'll be doing it!'

Three: Coningsby Park

It was, perhaps, unfortunate, that the next morning was grey and chilly. Coningsby was a house that required a good deal of sunshine to render it cheerful-looking. Against a leaden sky, it loomed, massive and forbidding. Its appearance was not improved by a row of gargoyles that leered down upon the visitors as they descended from their carriage, nor the two twisted towers at either end of the battlements, which had the appearance of leaning forward, ready to pounce.

Cecily shivered and clutched Dominic's arm as they stood upon the steps. The arrival of a perfectly ordinary and respectable butler to greet them reassured her, however, and she was emboldened to pass into what had been a medieval banqueting hall, which now functioned as the main reception room.

The walls of this apartment were panelled in blackened oak, hung with tapestries so ancient that the scenes they represented were indistinguishable, and further ornamented with the portraits of dead Guisboroughs, both male and female. Various swords, pikes, and maces were arranged in tasteful displays above the panels; and, to complete the comfort of the room, several suits of armour stood to attention along the walls.

'I can believe any horrors may be committed in this place,' whispered Cecily, unhappily. 'Poor Isabella.'

Dominic, who had left her side to inspect a pair of silver-mounted, flintlock duelling pistols from the previous century, displayed above the fireplace, merely laughed. 'My darling, if you knew nothing of the owners and were merely here to be shown over the place by the housekeeper, you would be in raptures.'

She smiled and admitted it to be so. 'Perhaps the rest of the house is a little more—homey.'

'I doubt it. In my experience, the British aristocracy is quite impervious to inconvenience, and the only comfortable apartments in the house are likely to be the housekeeper's room and the butler's pantry.'

At that moment, the butler returned. 'Lady Guisborough begs you will come up to her private suite, Ma'am,' he said with a bow. 'She is, unhappily, too unwell this morning to receive you downstairs. Miss Proudie—' here he sniffed contemptuously, '—will be along shortly to escort you to her.' He turned to Dominic and bowed again. 'My master is in the library, Sir, if you would allow me to conduct you.'

Dominic followed the butler through a massive door, turning on the threshold to clutch his own throat and pull a face of such terror that Cecily gasped. Then he winked at her, grinned, and sauntered after the servant. She giggled, her nervousness much abated.

A few moments later, she was completely reassured by the wholly conventional appearance of Miss Proudie, arrayed in decent grey bombazine. 'My dear Lady Cavendish. Thank you!'

'How is Isabella?' Cecily asked as they shook hands. 'The butler said she is feeling unwell.'

'Poor child, she is always unwell. But she has risen and dressed herself in preparation for your visit, which I hope will do her good. She is resting upon her sofa in front of the fire. I will take you to her.'

They left the great hall through a narrow door, which Cecily had not previously perceived. This led to a winding staircase, thence through a gallery with long windows looking out over the park, and eventually to a suite of rooms at the corner of the house incorporated into the tower, comprising a sitting room, a large bedchamber, and a dressing room.

Isabella was reclining upon a sofa in the sitting room. This was a charming apartment shaped rather like a slice of pie. The circular wall of the tower formed half the room, while the two walls made a wedge, at the apex of which was the fireplace. It was fitted up elegantly, but with great comfort, and in such a modern style that the antique shape merely added to its quaintness.

Cecily, seeing Isabella, so thin and pale, quite forgot her old school friend's elevated social position and ran to her. She fell on her knees beside the sofa and took the sick girl's hand in hers. 'Isabella—oh, I beg your pardon—Lady Guisborough—'

'Oh, do, please, call me Isabella. It has such a comfortable sound.' Isabella clasped Cecily's hand. Her fingers were so thin that it was like being gripped by a talon. 'It is lovely to see you again. I always thought you were the nicest of the older pupils. And the prettiest.'

Tears sprang to Cecily's eyes. 'I was well enough, but you—you were the most beautiful girl in the school.'

They began to talk of old times. Neither noticed when Miss Proudie quietly left the room. A few minutes later, a footman brought in a tray with Ratafia and little cakes.

'Pray, take some refreshment,' said Isabella, falling back upon her cushions with sudden languor.

'Will you have some?' Cecily picked up a glass and handed it to her. The girl took it, but her fingers shook.

'Thank you—if you would set it down for me.' She smiled uncertainly. 'You see how stupid and clumsy I am.'

'Dearest, you are ill. Will you not let me help you?'

Isabella shook her head. 'No one can help me. *She* wants me gone—you see.'

'She?'

'Lady Guisborough.'

'But, Isabella, you are Lady Guisborough.'

'No—not while she remains in this house.'

'She is dead,' said Cecily, bluntly.

'But not at rest.'

Cecily met those feverish eyes. 'Have you seen her?'

'Yes! Yes—many times. And she calls to me.'

'When did this begin?'

'Almost as soon as Guisborough brought me here.' She tried to smile. 'We had two months in Brighton after we were married—our honeymoon—and then—it began.'

'Dearest, is it not possible that your unhappiness—preying on your mind might—?'

'Unhappiness? What are you talking about?'

'Well,' Cecily hesitated. 'Miss Proudie said that you told her—you were—frightened—of your husband. When the proposal was first made, I mean.'

'No! Oh, no! That is all at an end. Oh, Cecily, you are a married woman, do I have to tell you how the love of a man—real, true love—'

'Oh?' Cecily was very much taken aback. 'You are happy—with him—then?'

'I love him with all my heart,' whispered Isabella.

'And he? Forgive me, but—does he return your affection?'

Isabella stared at her. 'Have I not just told you? His gentleness, his kindness—and then, when he had taught me to love him—his passion—! Oh Cecily, never doubt that my dear husband loves me.'

She lowered her voice and sent a furtive glance around the room that froze Cecily's blood. 'And that is why *she* hates me.'

****

Lord Guisborough was a man of five-and-thirty, of medium height and wiry build. His hair and eyes were very dark, the latter of considerable size and brilliance. He had a restless, intense manner that made Dominic's comparison with the actor Edmund Kean by no means unjust.

He came forward to greet his guest with his hand outstretched and a smile that did not reach his eyes upon his lips. 'Cavendish. Good of you to come!'

'Good of you to see me. You must be wishing visitors at Jericho. I hope Lady Guisborough's indisposition is not of a serious nature?'

'No! No, not at all! Pray, take a seat here by the fire. It is chilly this morning.' He picked up a paper that lay upon the table beside his chair. 'I had your letter. You tell me you are in Lincolnshire on very particular business. How may I assist you?'

Dominic had come prepared with a reasonable pretext for his visit. The matter was, indeed, one that he had discussed with his superiors, although not specifically in relation to Guisborough.

'Well, you probably know, Sir, that the government is concerned about increased revenue avoidance since the war. We are seeking the support of local landowners. You cannot, of course, be expected to police your own and your tenants' land—the area is too extensive—but, if we could have your permission for regular patrols, it would go far to diminish the trade in this particular neighbourhood.'

A gleam of humour stole into Guisborough's eyes. 'You ask me to make myself unpopular with the Gentlemen?'

'Their disapprobation can scarcely injure you, my Lord.'

The amusement vanished. 'No, nothing can injure me more than—' He lifted a hand in a gesture of agreement. 'Do as you wish, my dear fellow. You have my consent—and my very good will.'

He was silent for a moment and then cleared his throat in an embarrassed manner. 'You are quite lately married, I believe, Cavendish?'

'Almost two years now,' said Dominic with a grin. 'Time flies—as they say.'

'Truly? I have been married for six months, and it seems—a century!' The words seemed dragged from him. 'Do not misunderstand me. My wife is—an angel. I am blessed to have won her but, since we came down to Lincolnshire, she has been so unwell—' He paused; then it seemed that the comfort of unburdening his heart overcame his natural reticence. 'It is not her bodily ills. Those I could understand, comfort, and hope to alleviate. But—why should I prevaricate?—I have no doubt the tale is all over the county—it is her mind that is affected.'

Dominic said, with some compassion, 'Something of this I have heard, I confess.'

'She is obsessed with the idea that my first wife, my poor Caroline, wishes to be rid of her.' He dropped his head in his hands, and Dominic had to strain to hear his words. 'At our most—intimate—moments, she has started up crying that Caroline was—watching us! It has been weeks since—'

'My dear fellow, say no more, I perfectly understand you,' said Dominic hastily, blenching at the thought of further revelations.

Guisborough straightened his back and took a deep breath to steady himself. 'This is a very old house, indeed—some walls of the original Saxon manor remain. It has been rebuilt, added upon, for nearly a thousand years. Of course, there have always been rumours of—strange noises—objects moving without human agency, but I have never witnessed any such manifestations. Perhaps, as some claim, one must be sensitive. But, even if it were so, I cannot believe that Caroline—why, she was sweetness itself—'

Dominic debated within himself but decided it could do no harm to bring up the possibility of a human intelligence behind this haunting. 'Has it occurred to you that there may be some person who seeks to harm your wife—or you, through her—and that all these symptoms might be attributable to a purely physical cause?'

Guisborough looked up quickly, a sudden hope dawning upon his countenance. 'You think it possible?'

'More possible than a spiteful spirit or that an otherwise healthy young girl has lost her mind within a matter of months.'

'It has been suggested to me that the hysterical tendency was always there and that it is the shock of—physical passion—in fact—that has released it.'

Dominic raised his eyebrows. 'I beg your pardon, but that must be nonsense. If that were the case the country—indeed the world—would be overrun by mad women. Who said this to you?'

'A London doctor, Sir Willoughby Mountjoy. He explained that young women go through changes as they mature, and this can produce hysteria and—'

'But my dear Sir, your wife is a grown woman.'

'She is nineteen.'

'Had she been thirteen, your Sir Willoughby might have had some sense on his side; but then the case would not arise, as you would not have married her.'

'True. That is very much what my friend Hector Stewart, has said.'

'He is the attending physician?'

'Indeed. A very clever man.'

'What does he say of the matter?'

'He fears that there is something pressing upon the brain, producing hallucinations. But to discover what it may be would mean opening up her skull—it is too dangerous until all else has been tried.'

'Good God! I should think so, indeed.' Dominic was silent for a moment, considering what he had learnt. The explanation was certainly possible, even likely. But it did not explain why Isabella should have been found walking upon the very battlements where Guisborough's first wife had fallen to her death a few years earlier.

Guisborough interrupted the silence. 'Do you really think that there might be some—some malicious plot against my wife? That someone is deliberately inducing these manifestations?'

'I think it has to be considered. As a public man, we know you must have enemies. In a private capacity—only you can tell if you have injured any man so grievously that he would attack you through your wife.'

Guisborough frowned. He seemed to be passing late years under review to determine what injuries he might have caused. 'The difficulty is,' he said presently, 'not with one's intentions but the unforeseen results of one's actions. For example, not long ago, I wished to temporarily close down a mine on my property in Nottinghamshire. There was a problem with gas extraction, which I felt should be attended to before any more tunnels were dug. But men might have been thrown out of work for months— I was persuaded that the danger was slight and, so, to keep it open.'

'What happened?'

'There was an explosion. Dozens killed. I felt dreadfully about it.'

'That I can understand. But this could hardly be the work of an angry collier, my dear Sir.'

'No, of course not. I am trying to illustrate how seemingly well-meant actions may have consequences. One may cause harm without even knowing it.' He stood and began to pace the room, back and forth, as though his fevered brain must have an outlet. Suddenly, he stopped, wheeled upon his heels, and said, 'Help me, Cavendish. I know something of your history from the Minister. You have wrought in secret for your country's good. I beg you to use your talents to save my poor Isabella?'

Dominic met those brilliant, compelling eyes and read the despair in them. He could no more turn his back on this man than he could strike him down. 'Very well, Sir. I will do my best.'

Four: Sinner, Saint and Spy

From Coningsby Park, the carriage took Dominic and Cecily directly to Chertsey House. Cecily was inclined to become sentimental as they approached. It had been at a ball at Chertsey House that she had first understood her own heart and known that she loved Dominic, although, to be sure, she had no idea of his true identity. He had been a handsome and dangerous stranger—catching her up in his arms for a kiss and then off again on his adventures.

She turned to him, afire with love and romance, only to find that he had fallen asleep in the corner of the chaise, with his mouth hanging a little open. To her indignation, a tiny snore emerged from his throat. Then her heart melted. Poor darling Dominic. He worked too hard, the Minister was a brute, and she would not wake him for the world. But her woman's tenderness could not be completely denied. She leaned her cheek against his shoulder and covered one of his slackened hands with her own. Really, when she considered Isabella's suffering, she was the most fortunate of women, and would hardly admit that anyone could be as happy as she was—or at any rate—with so good a cause.

However, when Abby de Saint Michel came running forward to throw her arms around them both, she was forced to admit that here was a woman whose supreme happiness could not be doubted.

Abigail had features so regular, bones so delicately moulded, that her countenance was like a blank canvas upon which her emotions painted the picture. When she was distressed, lonely, or merely bored, she appeared rather plain. But now, with happiness and excitement making her eyes sparkle and her skin glow, she was quite beautiful.

'Dom! Cecily! Oh, I am so glad to see you!'

Dominic kissed her lips and hugged her shoulders. 'Hello, Abby. You're looking well. How does Raoul treat you?'

Abby was as tall as he, and her eyes beamed into his. 'Can you ask me? Raoul is the best husband in the world.'

'Thank you, *ma mie*,' said Raoul, coming up behind them. 'Since Dominic is kissing my wife, I shall take the liberty to kiss his.'

'You kissed her yesterday.'

'So I did. But I did not fully appreciate how very kissable she had become. Marriage agrees with you, my Lady Cavendish. I said it would.'

'Damned Frenchmen! Don't you ever think of anything else but—' He recollected that there were ladies present and changed what he had been about to say. 'Anything else but love?'

'Indeed, we do—at least I do. I have been thinking about making my fortune, and you, my dear Nick, are going to tell me how to do it, are you not?'

Dominic laughed. 'That takes me back. No one calls me Nick anymore.'

'People still tell stories about Young Nick,' interposed Abby. 'They grow wilder every day, so my father tells me. But no one knows the truth.'

'A fair number of the Gentlemen do.'

'They will never tell. They have their code.'

He threw back his head and laughed. 'As pernicious a bunch of scoundrels as ever I met. Believe me, Abby, they have no code. Just a wholesome fear of what I could tell the excise men if I chose.'

'You never did?'

'Lord no. They trusted me. You can't betray a trust, even—anyway, it was Raoul I was after.' He grinned at his former adversary. 'And I got him!'

'And let him go,' said Abby, smiling.

'What else could I do? If you could have seen your face—'

'That's enough, Dom,' said Abby, rendered uncomfortable by the memories he evoked. 'Come inside. You shall have a glass of sherry and then dinner.'

As they entered the cheerful, elegant, house, Cecily could

38

not help remarking how pleasant it was when compared to Coningsby Park.

'Oh? You have just come from there? How is the poor little Countess?' asked Abby, leading the way into the drawing room. 'I have never met her, of course, but the whole countryside is rife with the most outlandish rumours.'

Over an excellent sherry, Cecily recounted what they knew of Isabella's story. As she did so, a chill seemed to creep into the room, as though a shadow had fallen across their contentment.

'Poor, poor child,' said Abby when Cecily had finished. 'Do you think she is truly insane?'

'Dominic thinks it might be, as the doctor said, something pressing upon her brain.'

Raoul nodded. 'I have seen a head injury produce similar hallucinations. I watched once, after *la bataille de Mont-Saint-Jean*—'

Here Dominic mouthed 'Waterloo' at his wife, who mouthed back 'I know!'

'—while a surgeon removed a great piece of broken skull from a head wound. He bound the head and behold—the man was sane again!'

'That is wonderful!' cried Cecily.

'Indeed. He died a few hours later. But he died in his right mind.'

'Raoul!' said Abby reproachfully.

He looked at his wife, rather surprised. 'But what I say is true, *ma mie*.'

'I daresay.'

Cecily laughed. 'Don't be cross with Raoul. I know what he means. But perhaps it will not come to that. Do not forget the strange circumstances of his first wife's death. It is ludicrous to suggest that both Guisborough's wives should suffer from the same condition, and I, for one, believe that one person is behind her death and Isabella's illness.'

'That one person being—?'

'Why the Earl himself, of course.'

Dominic sighed. 'Darling, why? Just tell me that. Why would a man marry two beautiful girls within five years and murder them both in the most public and melodramatic way?'

'Well, perhaps *he* is the one with something pressing on his brain? Perhaps *he* is mad.'

'She has a point there, *mon cher* Nick,' said Raoul, judicially. 'Men have gone mad and killed their wives before now.'

'Well, if that is the case, I'm afraid poor Isabella is doomed. No one is going to suggest a man of Guisborough's wealth and position is a madman until he falls to raving in the House of Lords.' He thought about it and added, 'And they probably wouldn't notice, even then.'

Both the ladies cried out upon him, but the mood lightened. They fell to talking of old times until the butler called them in to an excellent dinner.

****

'And now, my very good friend, Nick,' said Raoul, as they returned to the dining table, having bowed the ladies out of the room in due form. 'Let us discuss this fortune you are going to aide me to acquire.' He picked up the decanter and courteously passed it to his guest. 'I fear this wine has paid no duty to the good King George.'

'I daresay.' Dominic sipped. 'Excellent port. The Squire has always been on good terms with the free-traders.' He sat for a moment and then, as though marshalling his thoughts, he began. 'Look Raoul, I don't know all your circumstances, but from what you said yesterday, and Abby has written to my wife—'

Raoul held up a hand. 'Do not attempt to be tactful. Let us agree, I need money—badly. And—' with a laugh, 'I would do almost anything—legal—to obtain it.'

'Oh, don't worry about that. My—or, rather, the Minister's—proposition is highly legal, even admirable.' He twirled the stem of the wineglass in his fingers. 'We know a lot more about you now, than we did a couple of years ago. It is true, is it not, that you were a younger son, and only became the heir to the Marquis de Saint Michel upon the death of your brother in a hunting accident?'

Raoul raised his eyebrows. 'It is. What of it?'

Dominic laughed. 'Forgive me. Is it also true that, before your brother's death, you sailed as captain of your own vessel, bringing goods back to France?'

Raoul frowned. 'Now, how did you find out about that? I sailed under another name. My family did not approve of a Saint Michel engaging in trade. Although they took my money readily enough to support them when they fled to England.'

'It doesn't matter how I know. I realised, of course, having sailed with you, that you were an experienced sea-captain; but I did not know the extent of your—voyaging.'

'Does all this have a point?'

'I am coming to it now,' said Dominic with a grin. 'Have you heard of the West Africa Squadron?'

Raoul sat up in his chair and set down his glass. 'Something,' he acknowledged.

'We want you to join,' said Dominic simply. 'We're building up the fleet, but it's a slow business; and, besides, the navy hasn't got your expertise in—shall we call it— skulduggery? The captains are inclined to go in flags flying, thus sending any slavers in the waters scuttling for cover. The Minister thinks that by engaging a former smuggler with experience in those waters, we could fight fire—with fire.'

'And when does this fortune you mentioned appear?'

'Firstly, you have the prize money for any captured slave ship. Secondly, a bounty for every freed slave. Lastly, any other cargo, ivory, spices, gold, is yours to keep and trade. Moreover, we will provide you with your vessel and crew.'

'It is almost irresistible.'

'Only—almost?'

'I am a married man. And one very much in love with his

41

wife. We have already been separated too much since our marriage.'

'I can understand that, of course. But I know my Abby. She would like nothing better than to sail with you.'

'Should I take her into danger?'

'Precious little danger. Those cowardly devils won't put up much of a fight. Not against you and the hand-picked men we plan to give you. Besides, you can leave her on shore on those nights you go hunting.'

'You tempt me very much,' said Raoul, his eyes kindling. 'It would give me great satisfaction to hang those evil men who batten on human flesh.' He sent Dominic a sharp look. 'I may hang them—*hein*?'

Dominic shrugged. 'A British naval captain at sea has the power of life and death. By all means, hang them from your yardarm—no one will miss 'em.'

'Is that you or your Minister talking?'

'Both.'

Raoul sank back into his chair, picked up the decanter, and poured more wine into his glass. 'I shall discuss the matter with my dear wife, *mon cher* Nick. I think we both know what her answer will be. And so I give you a toast—to freedom!'

Dominic lifted his own glass. 'Freedom!'

Five: Nurse Takes Charge

'What have you discovered about that unfortunate girl?' demanded the dowager Lady Cavendish that evening, as she sipped her tea, rather noisily, from her saucer. 'Is she off her head, as the servants say?'

'We don't know, Ma'am. There is something very wrong.' Dominic shot a questioning look at his grandmother. 'What do you think about it?'

'I? How should I know anything? I never leave this house.'

He laughed. 'I wouldn't ask if I did not know, from bitter experience, that nothing goes on between Lincoln and Skegness that you are not instantly informed of. Your network of spies would do credit to the War Office.'

She gave a grim laugh. 'Well—two mad wives is too much to swallow. There's spite at the back of it, if you ask me.'

'That is what I think too,' chimed in Cecily.

'Cecily thinks Guisborough is behind it,' said Dominic.

'It could be. There is instability in the family. His mother was a hysteric, no getting away from that!'

'I didn't know you knew her, Ma'am.'

'Aye, I knew her—knew the whole family, in fact. She was just such another as this little thing he's married. All the same, men—just looking for to marry their mothers.'

Dominic looked rather revolted. 'Cecily is nothing like my mother.'

'Keeps you in order, doesn't she?'

'Well—'

'Never mind that. If it's Guisborough, it will have to be hushed up.'

'I don't see why.'

'Country's going to the dogs as it is. Can't have the rabble thinking the nobility are going off their heads.'

'Most of them have been for years,' said Dominic, grinning.

'It is no laughing matter,' said his grandmother tartly. 'I have not forgotten what happened in France, even if you have. Some of my dearest friends went to the guillotine. All because the *canaille* took it into their heads that they were as good as their betters.'

'There was very great suffering among them,' ventured Cecily, who had read Rousseau and imbibed rather advanced ideas.

'I daresay. Well, the poor are always with us, as the Good Book says.'

'I talked with Guisborough,' said Dominic, bringing his womenfolk back to the point. 'I swear he is neither mad nor a murderer. He spoke of his wife with real passion and is in agony over her condition.'

'In such agony that he never goes to her chamber?' said Cecily in a sceptical tone.

Dominic was uncomfortable. He could not disclose the intimate details poor Guisborough had revealed, while the dowager was present. 'There are reasons.' He dropped his voice, 'I shall tell you later.'

'Oh, tell her now,' snapped old Lady Cavendish, whose hearing was as acute as ever it had been. 'I am tired and shall go to bed.'

Dominic at once jumped up to help the old lady to rise from her chair. She affected to be annoyed by his attentions but, as she left the room, she patted his cheek; and a softened expression came into her sharp, old eyes. 'You are a good boy,' she said. 'And I like your little wife. Now—make me a great-grandmother before I die, and I'll go a happy woman.'

'But we don't want you to go, Grandmother,' said Dominic, laughing it off, but conscious of Cecily, still seated at the tea table. He was just beginning to be aware of her unhappiness over her failure to conceive. She had been rather quiet after leaving Chertsey House and, when offered a penny for her thoughts, had said that Abby's baby was a dear little thing. It had been said with a sigh. For himself, he was very

44

content with things as they were. He had his Cecily all to himself, and there was little Bobby to play at cricket and catch balls with. Of course, in the future, they would have a fine family, of that he was sure. But there was no hurry.

He went back into the room and crossed to the bureau where the decanters stood in a gleaming row. 'Would you care for a glass of sherry or something?' he asked as he took up the brandy decanter.

'No, not for me, thank you,' she smiled and sank back in her chair. 'What was it you couldn't tell me in front of your grandmother?'

He poured a generous measure into his glass and came back to sit with his wife on her sofa. 'I'm not sure I should tell you; it may give you nightmares.'

'I am not such a poor creature.'

'Well, the case is that, when the poor fellow was—well— in the middle of—you know—'

She looked at him in some astonishment. 'No—I don't know. What are you talking about?'

Dominic took a deep breath. 'When he was in bed with Isabella, she thought she saw his dead wife watching them,' he said baldly.'

'Ugh! What a horrid thought! Poor, poor Isabella.'

'Poor Guisborough. I mean it would be guaranteed to put a fellow off.'

'Was it just the once?'

'No—I think not.'

'Then I sincerely pity him, if he is not the villain, after all.' She was silent for a few moments. 'I have been thinking—'

'Oh, Lord—again?'

'Really, Dominic—that is not funny. I have been thinking that we must call on Lady Fanshawe. We have been here two days already and not seen her or—'

'Or Peter?'

'I was going to say—or Nurse.'

'Ah, Nurse.' He laughed. 'Is it not a little pathetic how all we highly competent adults still turn to Nurse as the fount of all wisdom—and protection?'

'Well, she is,' said Cecily, in a reasonable tone. 'So it is not pathetic at all, but entirely sensible.'

Dominic stood and pulled his wife off the sofa and into his arms. 'I would rather you thought I was.'

'Was what?'

'The source of all wisdom and protection.'

She smiled up at him. 'I could not wish for any better protector—but—wisdom—hmmm?'

'Little cat.'

'That is what you called me the first time we met,' she remarked, winding her arms around his neck.

'Well, so you were.' He bent his head to kiss her. 'I like cats.' With that, he swept her up into his arms and, despite her giggling protests, carried her up the wide, oak staircase to their allotted bedchamber. And, if any shades of the departed Cavendish haunted the room that night, they went unnoticed.

****

'Cecily, my dear,' said Peter Fanshawe, descending the steps of Heron Lodge with his hand held out. 'Welcome back.'

Cecily, who had just been helped down from the dowager's barouche by her husband, accepted his hand with rather conscious formality. But she was unable, as ever, to resist his sweet, wistful smile, which made women long to comfort him—and most men long to kick him.

'Thank you, Peter. It is lovely to be here again. I can hardly believe it has been more than two years.'

'That long? Yes, of course, we were still in Bath on the last occasion that you visited Alford. After your wedding.'

There was a silence, then Cecily said, 'The Lodge looks very charming in the sunshine.'

'We have had a new coat of paint since you were here last, and a few other trifling renovations. Now that the trust money is not being—diverted—we have the wherewithal.'

'I am glad that some good has come of that awful time.' She heard Dominic, behind her, give a snort and hastily added, 'To you and Lady Fanshawe, I mean. Of course, it brought nothing but good to me.'

The wistfulness increased. 'Indeed, you are glowing with happiness. It gives me very great pleasure.' If he had added that it also gave him very great pain, his meaning could not have been more clear.

'Thank you,' she said again, rather inadequately. 'How is dear Lady Fanshawe?'

'My mother is as well as can be expected. She begs me to offer her apologies for not coming out to receive you. Will you come into the drawing room?'

'Of course.' A portly figure appeared in the doorway, and she gave a little cry of delight. 'Biggers! How glad I am to see you!'

'I venture to say, my Lady, as we are all very happy to welcome you. Mrs Nuttall has been in quite a flutter.'

'Oh, I must go and talk to her, after I have paid my respects to your mistress, of course. And Nurse, I must speak with Nurse.'

'Well, Miss—my Lady, I should say—you'll see Nurse right enough because she's sitting with the mistress this very moment. She won't be parted from Nurse for an instant. Quite childlike she's become.'

'Oh, I am so sorry.'

'Yes Miss—my Lady—but we don't have so much of the *other trouble*. If you take my meaning.'

Since the *other trouble* could only refer to Lady Fanshawe's predilection for strong spirits, Cecily was pleased to hear this, for the safety of the household, as well as for Lady Fanshawe's health.

She followed Biggers into the house while Dominic exchanged a few words with Peter Fanshawe.

They had been friends since boyhood, but the coolness

that had arisen, when each suspected the other of murder, had not yet been completely dissipated. And although Dominic knew perfectly well that Cecily had never been in the least in love with Peter, the knowledge that Peter had been, and possibly still was, in love with Cecily did not endear him to her husband.

Bigger threw open the door to the drawing room and announced, 'Sir Dominic Cavendish and Lady Cavendish, my Lady.'

'Oh, how I remember this room,' breathed Cecily, struck afresh by the pale-blue, satin upholstery, cream and gilt panels, the painted roses, and the plump, simpering cherubs. 'So beautiful!'

She ran forward to drop to her knees beside Lady Fanshawe, as exquisite as ever in a gown of stiff, pink brocade, with her white hair piled in curls on top of her head and a delicate spray of rosebuds adorning the lace fichu she wore, after the fashion of her youth.

The lady allowed her hand to be seized and smiled down at her visitor, a little vaguely. 'Why, it is Miss Danvers. Have you taken Robert for his walk this morning?'

'Now, Mama,' said Peter, who had followed Cecily into the room. 'You know very well that this lady is now Lady Cavendish and Bobby is living with the Leonards in Alford.'

'Do I?' She patted Cecily's cheek. 'You are a very good girl, Miss Danvers, and Robert is improving under your care. I hear you are teaching him French.'

'But Mama I just told you—'

At this point there arose, from a winged armchair beside the fire, the comfortable figure of an elderly woman, dressed all in black with a snowy muslin cap perched upon iron-grey hair.

'Don't argue with her, Mr Peter,' she said in a low voice. 'Talk about something else.'

Cecily had sprung to her feet at the sight of Mrs Harrison and now flung herself into her arms. 'Nurse! Oh, Nurse, I have missed you.'

'Have you, my pet? Well I am sure I've missed you, too. And you, Master Dom.' She lifted her cheek to receive Dominic's kiss and reached for his hand. She seemed to search his face, and a gleam of satisfaction came into her eyes. Whatever she had feared to see, it was no longer there. The shadow that had blighted Dominic's life for so long had quite lifted. She turned with renewed affection to the girl who had made her nursling such amends for all the tragedy in his past.

****

'Now, what is it all about?' said Nurse, settling herself comfortably in front of the fire in her own room. 'You're both full of some foolishness, I can see.'

'Have you heard—?' and: 'What do you think about—?' burst out of Dominic and Cecily simultaneously. They laughed. 'You tell it, Dominic,' said Cecily generously.

'It was you Miss Proudie appealed to—you tell it.'

'One of you better tell me!' commanded Nurse.

Cecily took a deep breath. 'Have you heard about Lady Guisborough's illness, Nurse?'

'Everyone has, my dear. Folks love a ghost story, and when it's a pretty young female is haunted—and another one doing the haunting—well, there's bound to be a lot of talk.'

'You don't believe in such things, do you, Nurse?'

'No, bless you, of course I don't. I won't deny that queer things happen, things a mortal can't explain, but the dead coming back to trouble the living—no. The Good Lord wouldn't allow it.'

'There, Dominic. So much for your exorcism idea.'

'You mean get a priest in?' Nurse nodded, considering. 'It might work.'

'But you just said you don't believe—'

'It don't matter what I believe. It is what she believes as counts. She may credit that a priest can drive away whatever visits her, and driven away it will be.' She got up and, opening a drawer, began to take out neatly folded garments. 'Master Dom, reach down that bandbox from the top of the wardrobe. You can drive me to Coningsby this afternoon.'

Cecily's mouth dropped open in astonishment. 'But—we haven't even told you what we want you to do.'

Mrs Harrison chuckled, and her eyes crinkled at the corners until they became almost slits. 'Bless you, my dear, as if I couldn't guess. You think the poor dear creature is being fed some horrible drug to make her imagine things that aren't there—and so do I. But, whoever it is, will have a hard job getting his nasty stuff past me, that's all!'

Six: Lady Cavendish Consults the Doctor

Rather to Cecily's surprise, Nurse was accepted by the servants at Coningsby Park with enthusiasm. Even the housekeeper, who might have been expected to bridle at the intrusion of another authoritative female, was found to have been trained in her first domestic position by Nurse and regarded her with profound veneration. Indeed, everyone, from the Earl down to the scullery maid, seemed to feel that 'Nurse would make everything better.' The only dissonant voice came from Lady Guisborough's French maid, and Mademoiselle Martin's opinion was generally held to be irrelevant as: 'She don't care 'bout nuffin' as ain't Froggie.'

By the time Cecily and Dominic left the Park that evening, Nurse was installed in the little dressing room off Isabella's bedchamber and engaged in brewing a posset over the fire, which, she said, would do her young ladyship the world of good. The little French lady's maid, a sharp-featured blonde, was bathing her mistress' forehead with vinegar, all the while casting looks of venomous dislike through the open door at Nurse's unconscious back. Even as she did so, Nurse remarked, as if to a naughty child, 'If the wind changes while you are pulling that face, it will stay that way forever.'

Marie-Claire started, went pale, and then quickly crossed herself.

Cecily hid a smile, for she could see, as Marie-Claire could not, that a polished silver vase on the dresser in front of Nurse perfectly reflected the maidservant's face. Well, let her think that Nurse had 'eyes in the back of her head,' as she had firmly believed her own nurse to have, when she had been little.

'Dear Isabella, we must leave you now. But I shall return to see how you do as soon as maybe,' said Cecily, leaning over the bed to kiss her friend's cheek. 'Nurse will look after you.'

Isabella managed a wan smile and returned the clasp on her hand. 'Thank you, dearest Cecily.'

Just as they were bidding Nurse farewell, there was a knock, and Lord Guisborough put his head around the half-open door. 'May I come in, my love?'

Isabella stretched out a trembling hand. 'Oh, Edward, is this wise?'

He stepped across the polished floor and sank to his knees beside her bed. 'You are my wife, Isabella. How can I leave you alone in your trouble?'

Marie-Claire drew back and cast a quick look around the chamber, as though she half expected to see the ghost of the dead Lady Guisborough rise up and cast his lordship from the chamber. Even Cecily felt a sudden superstitious chill. Then Nurse came bustling in from the dressing room with a steaming glass in her hand. 'Now, don't be a silly goose, my Lady. Of course, your good gentleman has come to see how you go on. Now you, Sir, just lift her up against the pillows and hold her while she drinks this posset down, and she will feel very much better. That's right, dearie, lean back against his Lordship's shoulder, and don't you be afeared. Nurse is here.'

****

'Really,' remarked Cecily as she sank onto the box of the barouche beside Dominic. 'Nurse is like a good fairy out of the storybooks.'

'A good witch, you mean,' he answered, giving his horses the office to move off. 'Why do you think they were all so delighted to see her? No spectral wife stands a chance against our Nurse's powers.'

'Dominic! How can you?'

'Did you not know?'

'You cannot seriously believe that darling old Nurse is a witch.'

'No, of course I don't. But the country people do. They treat her with the utmost respect—and caution.' He thought about it for a moment. 'And I must admit those possets of hers do work. I've swallowed quite a few of them myself.'

'I am sure she is extremely well versed in folk remedies,' responded Cecily with dignity. 'But I place more confidence in her sharp eyes and knowledge of human nature. I'll wager she sniffs out the truth in days, where it would take us weeks.'

'For Isabella's sake, I trust you are right.' Dominic had been briefly admitted to Lady Guisborough's sitting room and had been deeply shocked. 'I never met her when she was in good health, but anyone can see how frail she has become. And I fear her sanity is hanging by a thread. When we entered—she cowered.'

Cecily nodded, feeling herself unable to speak. Tears blurred her eyes. She wiped them away surreptitiously and cleared her throat. Dominic did not like to see her weep. 'I think it was because it is growing dark. In the morning, when I saw her last, she was fanciful but not, I think, fearful.'

'Very likely.' He cast a disparaging glance around him. 'If Guisborough cut a few of these trees down and opened up the prospect—not to mention ripping the ivy off those towers—it might improve matters. Anyone might imagine hidden terrors lurking in these shadows.'

'Well, if that isn't just like you, Dominic! I said practically the exact same thing when we were in the great hall, and you laughed at me.'

'I had not seen Isabella then. It is no laughing matter.'

'No. No, you are right. We must do something. No one else seems to be trying in the least.'

'Well, we have done something,' he pointed out. 'Our next move, it seems to me, is to interview the various persons on Kate's list.'

'But we have no authority to question anybody,' she reminded him.

'They won't know they're being questioned, Goose. People like to talk, you know, and they let fall all kinds of things they really should not—if they have anything to hide.'

She nodded. 'That is very true. Things just pop out when

one has a guilty secret.'

'When have you ever had a guilty secret?'

She dimpled. 'Oh, you do not know everything about my wicked past. When I was a little girl, I was quite naughty. And I was always caught because I babbled.'

He smiled down at her and put an arm about her shoulders. 'I wish I could have known you then. You must have been adorable.'

She leant her head against his arm. 'You would have called me skinny and pulled my hair and probably put beetles down my back.'

'Never! Even as a lad I was a perfect gentleman.'

'That is not what Abby and Kate say.'

'Oh?' He shifted a little uneasily in his seat. 'What have they been telling you?'

'Oh, lots of things. Like the time you tied Abby to a tree and did a war dance around her with turkey feathers stuck in your hair. And, once, you dangled Peter off the old clock tower until he admitted he had cheated at something or other; and—'

He grinned. 'I was a cursed young brute. However, Peter deserved it. He was umpire and called me *out* when I was most definitely *not out* because he was scared of what the village team might do to him. We were winning, and they didn't like it.'

'We?'

'The Gentlemen.'

She was startled. 'You had a team of smugglers?'

He threw back his head and laughed. 'No, no, sweetheart! In cricket, the Gentlemen are the—well—gentlemen, and everyone else the "players," you see.'

'The mysteries of cricket are beyond me; but, whatever he did, it obviously still rankles.'

'I hate to lose,' he said, whipping up his horses. 'I say, I'm devilish hungry. Aren't you?'

She nodded. 'I must admit I'm looking forward to my

dinner. Your grandmother's Mrs Skelton is a wonderful cook. Do you think she would give me the recipe for her lobster tarts?'

'I think you would have to prize it out of her with thumbscrews. But I expect I can persuade her.'

'Dominic, have you always been irresistible to women?' she asked, tucking her hand into his, and snuggling closer.

'Always. Look how you fell in love with me in an instant,' he said in a teasing voice.

'Is it something you can—snuff out? I don't want other girls falling in love with you.'

He bent his head and kissed away her pout. 'As a matter of fact, they're always doing it. I don't take any notice.'

Outraged, she boxed his ears—so he kissed her again—as a consequence of which, their return home was very much delayed.

* * * *

Lady Cavendish smiled at her husband across the breakfast table. He was just finishing his third cup of coffee; therefore, she judged, he could reasonably be drawn into conversation.

'Who shall we question first, do you think?'

'From your tone, I fancy you have already made up your mind about it,' he answered with a grin.

'Yes. I think we should begin with the doctor.'

'And why have you come to that conclusion?'

'Well, he is best placed to administer drugs and, therefore, very possibly the culprit—and if he isn't—he is the most likely person to have noticed something that can help us.'

He considered this. 'True enough. I shall have to conjure up a few symptoms for his entertainment.'

'Nonsense. It is obvious I should be the one with the symptoms. Women have all kinds of vague disorders I can lay claim to.'

'I'm not going to let you be examined by a strange doctor

who might be a homicidal maniac! What do you take me for?'

She blushed. 'Oh, I shall not discuss anything—anything—intimate. Just low spirits and—and—sleeping badly. Things like that.'

'Nevertheless, I will be with you during this consultation.'

'I think I should do better alone.'

'No! And that is my final word on the subject!'

That afternoon, when Doctor Stewart's gig turned into the driveway, Dominic was sitting in Kate's parlour complaining about women's obstinacy in general and his own wife's in particular.

Cecily received the doctor in a little used salon on the ground floor, a dark, chilly apartment furnished in the sombre style of Queen Anne. Cecily had deliberately worn a gown of thin, lilac cambric, as a result of which, she was shivering. Moreover, the chamber had once been the family chapel and boasted a stained-glass window. Cecily had noticed that, when light shone through the window, the blue, green, and purple glass cast a ghastly pallor on anyone sitting below it. Any doctor worth his salt, she considered, would instantly prescribe a tonic.

Her first thought, when the doctor entered the room, was that he was quite extraordinarily handsome. His hair, which he wore rather long, was of a colour that could only be described as golden. His eyes were a bright, cornflower blue, and his chiselled features would have graced a statue of Apollo. He came forward to shake her hand with a pleasant, professional smile; and Cecily was, most unreasonably, instantly convinced that he could not be the poisoner.

When he spoke, he had a slight but pleasing Scottish accent. 'Now, what did you want to consult me about, Lady Cavendish? Nothing serious, I hope.'

Cecily, who was rarely ill, answered in a weary, peevish tone, quite unlike her own. 'Oh, I am never well when we come into Lincolnshire. I do not think the climate suits me. It weakens my constitution and, as a result, I am chilled to the bone, even now, in the middle of the summer.'

'Well, we are having a very poor summer, it is true.' He looked at her and gently suggested a shawl might alleviate her situation.

'Oh, it is not that. I vow I have not slept a wink all week. And I have dreadful dreams.'

'But, dear lady, if you have dreams, you must have slept.'

She disregarded this interruption. 'I have a very sensitive nature, and the least little thing discomposes me. Ever since I learned of the awful happenings at Coningsby Park, I have been able to think of nothing else.'

'Do you refer to Lady Guisborough's indisposition? I understand you have visited her twice. Her complaint is not communicable, I assure you.'

She had forgotten that he would be aware of her connection with Isabella. She achieved a convincing shudder and, dropping her voice, she said, 'Dear Isabella has told me—I vow my blood ran cold when she said she had encountered that horrid spectre.'

'I think, perhaps, you two young ladies have been frightening each other in the manner of children telling ghost stories when they should be asleep.'

'You do not believe she has seen—it?'

'My dear lady, I am a man of science. I have noted over and over that people—particularly fanciful young ladies—see what they expect to see. I have no doubt the lady has seen a shadow—a shimmer of light, perhaps—and has constructed her spectre from that.'

'But the ghost led her out of her chamber, onto the battlements, and across the park to the family tomb. If these are hallucinations, then surely—'

He shook his head and interrupted her. 'Forgive me, Lady Cavendish, I cannot discuss my patient's case with you, any more than I would discuss yours with her.'

Cecily subsided, looking crushed. She allowed a slight quaver into her voice as she said, 'I know and I do respect your—your—professional scruples. But we are such very old friends. We were at school together, you know.'

He smiled. 'I had heard so. If I may say so, the standard of feminine beauty at that establishment must have been extraordinarily high.'

'Why, Doctor! Is it professional to pay your patients compliments?'

'I do not think you are my patient, Lady Cavendish. In fact, I do not think you are sickly at all. You sent for me because you are worried about your friend and hoped to glean some information on her condition from me.'

There was an uncomfortable silence, and then Cecily's mischievous smile made its appearance. 'You are perfectly right, Doctor Stewart. My poor Isabella is strangely alone in that big house. I want to help her if I can.'

'She has her husband.'

'Forgive me, but he seems to make her worse.'

He sighed as though to acknowledge the truth of this.

'The Earl told my husband you think the trouble may be physical. Something pressing on the brain.'

'I really cannot discuss it wi' ye, Ma'am,' he rejoined becoming more Scottish in his exasperation 'Why canna women take no for an answer?'

'Then tell me, did you know the Earl's first wife— Caroline?' He was silent, and she said in her most persuasive manner, 'It is not idle curiosity, Sir, I swear. But, as the poor lady is dead, surely the confidentiality of your profession does not apply.'

He shrugged. 'Aye, I knew her.'

'What was she like?'

He was silent for a moment, and then, as though the words were forced out of him, he said, 'She was a—beautiful— gentle—creature. Too good for this world.'

'Like Isabella? Do you think there is a connection?'

'I told you, Ma'am, I am a man of science. How can there be any connection?'

58

'Did she also—see—things?'

'The poor wee lady swore she could hear sobbing in the dead of night, but I do not think she ever claimed to see anything. There has always been talk. It is the same with any ancient house. There is a cavalier's widow supposed to walk the battlements you know.'

'Sobbing?' Cecily did not have to feign a shudder.

'Aye, the lady's husband and three sons all died at Naseby. She threw herself from the battlements when the news was brought to her. To my mind, it is just the howling of the wind that produces the sound.'

'Poor Lady Guisborough. I should think that would prey on anybody's nerves.'

'Many a cottager's wife must have died o' grief in those days. Do they all walk? No, it is only where there are long, echoing corridors and auld ruins that these ladies canna rest, it seems.'

She smiled. 'You are very reassuring, Doctor Stewart. You know, having brought you out on a spurious errand, the least I can do is offer you some refreshment. Won't you have a glass of wine and a slice of cake with me? To show there are no hard feelings?'

He laughed. 'I should be glad of something to eat, I confess. I came here straight from a confinement in the village and have had nothing all morning.'

'Oh, then you must have more than cake! I know there is an excellent game pie in the larder, and half a cold roast pheasant.'

He relaxed into his chair. 'Well, I must say, a mouthful of pie would be very welcome, very welcome, indeed.'

'And perhaps a flagon of ale to wash it down.'

'Lady Cavendish—your husband is a fortunate man!'

By the time Doctor Stewart sat down to his belated repast, Cecily had ordered the fire to be made up and candles brought, for the afternoon was dark with threatening storm clouds. The doctor glanced out of the window and remarked, 'My anthophilous will be making their way home. They always know when there is a storm coming.'

'Anthophilous?'

'Bees, Ma'am. Beekeeping is my hobby.' He gave a deprecating little laugh, 'Or, rather, my obsession.'

'How—how interesting—and unusual.'

'There speaks the town-bred woman. I am not the only beekeeper in this part of the country, I assure you. We all vie wi' each other at the village fete. There's a prize for the best-tasting honey. I'll send you a jar of mine; it is very good for a "weakened constitution."'

She smiled at this mild jibe and said, 'How did you come to settle here? You are from Scotland, are you not?'

'Aye, from Inverness. My family inhabit a crumbling castle even older than Coningsby. Hence my familiarity with ghoulish legends. There's a tale that an ancestor of mine ran riot with a claymore and dispatched his entire family in a rage o'er a dish of burnt porridge!'

'Goodness! And do their ghosts haunt the castle?'

He chuckled. 'The only spectres that haunt the castle are black beetles and dry rot, my Lady. My poor parents are martyrs to the rheumatics.'

'How did they feel about your becoming a doctor?'

'Not happy, not happy at all. My father wanted me to go into the army, my mother—the church. To them, a medical man is on a par with an upper servant. However, I was the youngest son and of no real interest or value, so I was allowed to have my way. Fortunately, my old friend Guisborough encouraged me set up in this neighbourhood, and there's no doubt his patronage helped me to become established.' He put down his napkin and picked up the tankard. He drained it and set it down. 'My sister will be worrying if I'm caught in the storm. I must be getting on. I have to thank you for a very pleasant visit.'

'Your sister? I did not know she lived with you.'

'Aye, she's a wee delicate thing, and the rigours of life in the castle didna just suit her. So she keeps house for me. We look after each other, as you might say.'

'Does she go out? To parties—balls?'

'Och, there are precious few of those in this part of the country. She's happiest at home with her books and her needle.'

He stood and walked to the door. 'I can see myself out.' But this she could not allow. As she walked with him to the door, she said, 'Is there really nothing else in your doctor's bag that will help my poor Isabella?' She smiled in her most coaxing manner. 'We are all so worried about her.'

'Nothing but strengthening foods—cream, eggs, honey, liver, and sweetbreads. That is the best medicine.'

'Not all in the same dish, I hope,' remarked Cecily with a chuckle.

Seven: The Priest's Tale

In accordance with Dominic's instructions, when she had seen the doctor drive away, Cecily returned to the drawing room and took out a tablet, upon which she proceeded to note down what she considered the salient points of the interview.

When her husband returned, soaked to the skin, she barely allowed him time to remove his wet coat and toss off a bumper of brandy to ward off a possible cold in the head, before she sat him down in front of the fire with what she proudly called her 'report.'

'Well, let's see what kind of a Runner you would make,' he said, with a chuckle. He studied the paper carefully and then looked up. 'You think the doctor was in love with the Earl's first wife. Why?'

'He could not bring himself to speak her name, while Isabella was always "Lady Guisborough".'

He looked amused. 'Is that all?'

'No, it was the tone of his voice when he talked about her.'

'In other words, you are just guessing.'

'Well, that is all either of us can do.'

'True enough. You mention that he called himself a man of science twice. Why is that significant?'

'*Methinks the doctor doth protest too much*!' she laughed. 'And, surely, as a man of science, he should be investigating these phenomena, not just dismissing them.'

'Possibly.' He read on down the page. 'Not very well off, you think? But what could he gain from Lady Guisborough's death.'

'I was just putting down my impressions, as you told me to.'

He grunted and went back to the paper. 'He seems a very harmless individual. To sum up, he is a country doctor with very little cash or property, dependent upon the patronage of his much wealthier friend. He was in love, so you say, with his patron's wife. Oh, and he keeps bees. Is there a reason for murder in any of this?'

'Not unless he is insane.'

'Even a madman must have some logic to support his delusions. Or so I have heard.'

'Perhaps Caroline spurned him?'

'Then why seek to harm Isabella?'

'Perhaps you are right and it is the Earl who is the actual target—that someone is attacking him through his wives. Perhaps he really hates Lord Guisborough and—'

'If he hated him, why not simply move to another part of the country? Hatred hardly ever leads to murder, you know. Not unless it is combined with a very real injury.'

'What injury could the Earl have done him? He seems to have been a very good friend.'

Dominic laid down the paper and leaned back in his chair. 'Well, we should certainly investigate the good doctor's background. I can get the department on it to see if anything is known about him. But, on the surface, I would say he is just what he seems to be.'

Cecily settled back in her chair and gazed into the fire. After a few moments, she said, 'Kate said that we should look for who had the opportunity and worry about the "why" later. Well, it seems as though just about everyone in Lincolnshire had the opportunity. So let's think about the purpose behind all this. You say hatred does not lead to murder. So, what does? What possible object can there be to justify all this— well, not justify—but you know what I mean.'

'I am no expert, sweetheart, whatever Miss Proudie believes. But, if I had to hazard a guess, I should say— excluding the kind of bloodlust that kills for the sake of it— money, frustrated passion, and revenge.'

'Well, let us take the first item on the list. Money. Does anyone—anyone at all—come into money if Isabella dies?'

He shook his head. 'I cannot think so. Her family are poor as the proverbial church mouse, of course, and the father, by all accounts, is pretty unscrupulous. But he is far more likely to benefit while she is alive and may be applied to for assistance.'

'Very well. And, if we say it is the Earl who is the eventual target, who inherits Coningsby if he dies?'

'That I don't know. Stay, Grandmother has a copy of Debrett's Peerage in the library. That will tell us.' He lounged out of the room and returned with a leather-bound volume. It took only a few moments to find the correct entry.

'Here we are: Edward, fourth Earl of Guisborough, married Caroline, daughter of Sir Simon Hazeltine Bart, died 1811, no issue—Ah—heir apparent Michael Edward Sullivan, son of Maria Coningsby, granddaughter of the second Earl's youngest brother—so some kind of cousin—born 1808. That's him—that's our murderer—an eight-year-old boy!'

'His mama and papa are not eight years old,' Cecily reminded him.

'According to this, they reside in County Cork.'

'There are such things as ships, dear Dominic.'

'We have heard nothing of any strangers in the neighbourhood.'

'Pooh, that is nothing. They could be living in Lincoln or Nottingham.'

'My dear girl, how do you suppose one or other was able to slip poison into Isabella's cup from Lincoln or Nottingham?'

'Well, quite obviously, they would have a—a— conspirator in the house.'

'If you say so. It is a highly unlikely theory, but we can bear it in mind. Now, what about frustrated passion?'

She sighed. 'That is very complicated. Passion for who?'
'Whom.'

'Do not be pedantic, darling.' She knit her brows. 'Is it someone who loved Caroline and determined that, if he could not have her, no one should? Or someone who loved Guisborough and wanted Caroline out of the way? Or was

Caroline's death truly a tragic accident and is it someone who is madly in love with Isabella?'

'This is all very Shakespearian, but I don't believe a word of it. It is too farfetched.'

Cecily nodded regretfully. 'I think that, too. So we are left with—revenge.'

'I talked to Guisborough about that. I can tell you this— if he has wronged someone so severely that he and his loved ones must be driven to madness and suicide—he is quite oblivious of it.'

'Perhaps it was his father who injured someone. You know "the sins of the fathers" and all that.'

'Well, that lets out the doctor. The old Earl was already dead when Stewart and Guisborough met at school.'

Cecily gave a little shrug. 'Oh, well, it is getting late, and we must dress. We can decide what to do next after dinner.'

Dominic looked at her rather meaningfully. 'I know what I would like to do next,' he said with a laugh in his voice.

'Oh, darling,' she replied, and forgetting all about the Guisborough family mystery, she walked into his arms.

* * * *

They had decided, when they could bring themselves to turn their minds once more to crime, that the next unsuspecting candidate for the role of murderer should be the Reverend Mr Tweedie. There could be no difficulty about this. Mr Tweedie's church, Saint Martin's, was both ancient and historically significant. Visitors were shown the damage to the walls left by the Parliamentarians' musket balls after the Battle of Winceby. The verger would display the marks left by their pikes on the wainscoting and the bloodstains, which, he would relate in a hushed voice, had been washed out over and over but always returned the next day.

Dominic and Cecily, however, did not avail themselves of the verger's services. They came armed with a note of introduction to Mr Tweedie from Lion Leonard and purposely arrived just after matins so that they might be sure of finding the vicar at home.

Lion had laughed when asked for the note and said, 'You won't need it, old fellow. Not with Cecily in that hat. Tweedie still has an eye for the ladies.'

Cecily did, indeed, look very pretty that morning. Blissfully happy and assured of her Dominic's devotion, which had been most amply demonstrated the night before, she was radiant in an Angouleme bonnet, trimmed with silk violets and fluttering satin ribbons. Her stylish driving dress fashioned in a deep-cream, ribbed silk, and an embroidered, cashmere shawl, the gift of the Marquis de Saint Michel—the provenance of which she did not enquire into—was draped negligently across her elbows.

So enchanting was the vision she presented that the vicar, espying their barouche from his window, emerged from the house like a jack-in-the-box, wreathed in smiles.

The Reverend Mr Tweedie's appearance came as rather a surprise to Cecily. For some reason, perhaps because Tweedie suggested 'weedy,' she had envisioned a tall, thin, scholarly gentleman, perhaps with a permanent student's stoop and half-moon spectacles. But the Reverend was a hale and hearty man of early middle-age, with a thick mane of greying hair and a high colour that betokened a love of—probably smuggled—port.

'This is a pleasure, a real pleasure,' he cried in a rich, pulpit voice. 'Come in and let me offer you some refreshment. I take it you wish to see over the church? Well, the church is not going anywhere, so let us first take a glass of something to warm us and a little bite of luncheon after.'

The living of Saint Martin's was in the gift of Guisborough. Here was another old friend who owed his prosperity to the Earl. And it was obvious that the living was a good one. The parsonage was a fine, mansion-like building constructed in the last century from the local cream-coloured limestone. Inside, all was comfort, reflecting the tastes of an unmarried, sporting, clergyman. Hunting prints adorned the walls, deep armchairs invited repose, and a strong smell of tobacco pervaded the upholstery, bearing testament to the solace of Mr Tweedie's solitary evenings.

When they were ushered into the little dining parlour, however, Cecily was glad to find the air fresh and perfumed with a bowl of roses rather than pipe tobacco.

'Tell me, how is my friend Leonard—and his good lady, of course?' He continued, giving them no time to answer, 'I have not seen him since—oh, it must have been last Easter when we took a service together—no—I tell a lie—it was June quarter day on the Feast of the Baptist in the Cathedral, and dinner afterwards with the Bishop. An excellent dinner it was, too. The Bishop is a hospitable fellow and exceedingly amiable, considering his attainments and connections.' He ran on in this way with a garrulity that spoke either of a man with nothing to hide—or a very clever actor.

When he eventually paused for breath, Cecily ventured a question, hoping to set him off again in the right direction. 'Have you been the incumbent of Saint Martin's for many years, Sir?'

'Ten years, my dear lady. Ten very happy years. I was offered the living by my friend Guisborough on my return from India in the year Six.'

'Oh? You were in India? How interesting. Do tell—'

Mr Tweedie needed no encouragement. 'Aye, I was fortunate enough to be offered a chaplaincy in the East India Company when I left Coningsby Park.

Dominic looked up quickly, then said in a deliberately casual voice, 'You were living at the Park then, Sir?'

'I had the honour to be the young Earl's tutor and mentor until he went up to Oxford. I was obliged to seek—that is—I was at a loose end and thought a stint in the East would be an agreeable change. Oh, that was the life I can tell you! The sport, the society—'

'You must have learned a lot about the East, its customs,

its native cuisine—herbal remedies—' Cecily remarked suggestively.

'Oh I left all that to the missionary fellows. I only went off the cantonments for the hunting, or if one of the local bigwigs gave a reception for the officers. Very decent fellows, some of the local princes, *maharajas* they call them. Never see the wives, though, just the *Nautch* girls. They could teach our opera dancers a thing or two, I can tell you.'

Normally, Dominic would have deprecated this loose talk in front of his wife. But it was no part of his plan to shut the vicar up, and so he let him ramble on.

'It sounds wonderful,' Cecily breathed, her eyes round with admiration. 'How I envy you. What I would not give to ride on one of those wonderful elephants. Whatever induced you to leave India and come back to tedious little England?'

The vicar's face altered in an instant. He had lost himself in talking about his experiences; now his face was shuttered, secretive. It was apparent to Dominic and Cecily that his departure had been sudden and probably compulsory. 'Well, you came to take a tour of the church, not to listen to me,' he said. 'Shall we go?'

The church aroused Cecily to genuine interest, particularly the indissoluble bloodstains. There were also some crusading Coningsbys in marble sarcophagi and some tattered banners betokening the family's more recent martial exploits in the Civil War, which were well worth looking at. Dominic inspected the famous musket ball craters in the ancient stone and privately gave Cecily his opinion that they dated from a later period than the mid sixteen hundreds. 'More likely, the Gentlemen using the church to store run cargo got into a fight.'

Presently, Mr Tweedie recollected that he had work to do and, after shaking hands with Dominic and kissing Cecily's hand with unexpected gallantry, he departed.

'Well,' said Dominic as they watched the reverend gentleman hurry back to his house. 'What next?'

'Let us examine the graveyard where poor Isabella was found that night.'

'What do you expect to find? Scorch marks in the shape of a demon's hoof, or the bones of a murdered nun?'

'Very funny! I do not know that I expect to find anything. I just want to see it.'

He took her hand and tucked it into the crook of his arm. 'Whatever you wish. Far be it from me to dampen your enthusiasm for tombs.' He looked up at the darkening sky. '*Dampen* being the right word. I should think the storm will break any minute. It's just the afternoon to go wandering around a graveyard. Delightful! We can take shelter in the family crypt.'

'What did you think of the vicar?' said Cecily as they strolled towards the corner of the graveyard where the Guisborough family vault lay.

'I'd like to know why he had to leave India.'

'Yes, so should I. I'm disappointed. I thought perhaps he might have meddled with some Eastern poisons or drugs out there, but if he never went off the cantonment—'

'So he says. You mustn't believe everything you are told.' He reached up to swat at a bee that was buzzing around his head, then another, and another. 'What the devil—?'

'Look, over there beyond the fence. Beehives! Doctor Stewart must have been talking about the vicar when he said he wasn't the only beekeeper in Coningsby.'

'Unless those are the doctor's hives. Does he live near here?'

'How in the world should I know? They are very persistent aren't they? The doctor said that bees are affected by stormy weather.'

'Well, they have been having a very agitating summer then.'

By this time, they had reached the crypt. It was built of the local marble, but Cecily thought the gothic structure would have been more appropriately constructed of crumbling

69

granite. 'It looks like a very small cathedral,' she remarked. 'I count six spires and four flying buttresses, which is a little excessive for a structure the size of a shed.'

'I agree it's devilish ugly, but does it suggest anything to you?'

'No, not yet. Can we get inside?'

Dominic put his hand against the wrought-iron bars within the arched doorway and pushed. It opened with well-oiled ease. He bent his head and looked around. There were several caskets stacked against the walls. One, which had the appearance of being the most recent, was adorned by an urn filled with the sweet, humble flowers that might be found in any cottage garden—daisies, asters, and pinks.

'That must be Caroline's,' whispered Cecily, following him inside. 'Who do you suppose—?'

'I don't know, but someone has not forgotten her. Perhaps it's your lovelorn doctor friend.'

'Whoever it is, I'm glad she is still mourned,' said Cecily softly. 'She died so young.'

Eight: Sed Exorcismus

They returned to Maythorpe Manor to find Lion Leonard awaiting them. He emerged from the front door as the barouche swept into the drive and greeted Dominic with a grin. He waved a piece of paper at him. 'It came this morning from the Bish. He is willing to let us try an exorcism.'

'Excellent!' Dominic sprang down from the barouche. 'When will he be here?'

'Who—he?'

'The exorcist, of course.'

'I am the exorcist, my dear fellow,' grinned Lion. 'But, you know, it is not what our brethren in Rome would consider an exorcism. I shall read a prayer of deliverance and command any earthbound spirits to depart in the name of our Lord. All very tame and decorous.'

Cecily, realising that her husband had forgotten all about her, climbed down from the barouche without assistance. 'Have you ever done one before?' she asked as she kissed Lion's cheek in a sisterly fashion.

'No, but that's all right. As I said, we do not, in the Anglican Church, have specially trained priests for the work. And it is not as though I have to deal with a case of demonic possession or anything of that nature.'

'No, indeed. It is as though all the spirit has departed from Isabella rather than entering into her.'

'Is it so indeed,' said Lion suddenly grave. 'If I can give her any comfort—'

Dominic looked up as a thought struck him. 'Do you know if Guisborough has sought any help from the Church before?'

'I am fairly sure he has not.'

'That is odd, when you come to think of it.'

Lion shrugged. 'He is a modern thinker. A man who trusts in learning, not faith. He has turned to the medical profession, rather than to religion.'

Dominic looked at his wife. 'Did I not see a crucifix in

Isabella's room?'

'Did you? I should not be surprised. Her family is very High Church, I believe. Incense, and Latin, and all that.'

'I trust she has been offered some spiritual comfort,' said Lion with a concerned look. 'Mr Tweedie—?'

'I don't think Mr Tweedie would be her idea of a spiritual comforter,' said Cecily with a sniff.

Dominic shrugged. 'He would not be mine, either. I should say he would be good for christening, marrying, and burying, but not much else. But what I meant was—will Guisborough consent? Whatever his wife's feelings may be.'

Lion gave this his consideration. 'If I were in his position, I would grasp at anything that might give comfort, whether I had faith in its efficacy or not. But there is only one way to find out. We must ask him.'

'You and I can ride over tomorrow morning and talk to him. Come to think of it, I don't know why he should object. He did ask for my help, after all.'

'What about me?' demanded Cecily, looking at her husband with sharp suspicion.

'I think it would come better from me—and Lion—man to man.'

'I want to see Isabella, and Nurse.'

Dominic frowned. 'I don't like you going over there. There may be—oh, I don't know—danger of some kind.'

'With Nurse around?'

'Oh, very well. Lion, we'll meet you there. Will eleven o'clock suit you?'

'Certainly. I'll send a note over to Coningsby to let the Earl know to expect me.'

So it was that the three men were gathered together in the Earl's library the next morning while Lion, with all the tact of which he was capable, put his argument.

'You see, Guisborough, it is a matter of atmosphere. Your household is in turmoil; there is fear of the unknown, the uncanny. It cannot be helpful to your wife's condition. And she herself might find—comfort—if she places herself under the protection of the Church.'

Guisborough said nothing for a moment. He stood reading the bishop's letter and then absently pulled on the bell-rope. When a liveried footman came in answer to the summons, he said, 'Is Doctor Stewart still in the house?'

'Yes, my Lord.'

'Ask him to come in here for a moment, would you?'

'Yes, my Lord.'

When Stewart appeared, Guisborough put the proposal to him. 'What do you think?'

'As a rational man, I think it is bunkum,' responded the doctor with a grin. 'Saving your presence Reverend, prayer is of very little use against a tumour. But, if you are asking if it will help to lift Lady Guisborough's melancholy, then, yes, I think it might ease her mind.'

The Earl nodded in a thoughtful manner. 'I can see that—yes—if a mind is sufficiently credulous to believe in spirits, it might believe in—' He broke off with an apologetic glance at Lion Leonard. 'Not that I mean to equate the two, of course.'

'I assure you, my dear Sir, there is no "bell, book, and candle" in the offing. Merely a prayer of protection in our Lord's name.'

The Earl glanced at Doctor Stewart, who gave a decided nod. 'Aye, what harm can it do?'

'Then, there is no time like the present. Let us proceed.'

'One moment, Guisborough,' demurred the doctor. 'I really think I should be present, as Lady Guisborough's medical advisor. Could you delay it for an hour or so? I have to dress little Betty Struthers' bad leg. It pains her, poor child. And I must warn my sister that I may not be able to dine with her. She worries, you know. I can ride over to the village and be back by noon.'

Lord Guisborough nodded absently, then said to Lion, 'Do you think, perhaps, Mr Tweedie, might assist?'

Lion admirably concealed a grimace. Whatever his own

view of the Vicar of Saint Martin's, the Earl had every right to ask him to be present if he so desired. 'Certainly, if you wish it.'

* * * *

It was just after noon that the little group assembled in Lady Guisborough's triangular bedchamber. Nurse was allowed to remain, but Cecily and Miss Proudie had been turned out of the room in no uncertain manner. There remained Guisborough, the doctor, and the two clergymen.

The Anglican exorcism was nothing more than a simple, but beautiful, prayer of protection and peace. Lion read it well, and the plain, dignified words seemed to exercise a beneficial effect upon the patient. Her big eyes grew calm, and the premature lines between her brows were smoothed away.

Then, as his beautiful voice declaimed, "*May she, fearing only you, have no other fear,*" there came a sudden blast from the fireplace. A black cloud issued forth as billowing smoke, yet the fire had died to embers. There was an unearthly sound, whirring, hissing pulsing around them like all the fires of Hell let loose. The cloud shot towards Lion and, within moments, he was covered in a black, heaving mass.

'My God! What the—!' Dominic was momentarily stunned. He ran forward but was pulled back by the doctor.

'Leave this to me, man! That is no demon spirit. It is bees—they're swarming. Don't move, Leonard; they won't sting if you don't threaten them.'

But Lion, like any layman, was beating at the insects, desperate to fend off the terrifying cloud that enveloped him. 'Open all the windows,' called the doctor. 'Tweedie, you know what to do!'

Dominic recollected that both men were amateur beekeepers. He stepped back to allow them to do what they must, trusting with all his heart that they knew what they were doing.

Apparently, they did. The Reverend Tweedie dragged a

cover from the bed and threw it over Lion's head. The bees angrily flew out from under the cloth while Doctor Stewart ran to the fireplace, hurriedly filled a shovel with hot coals, threw something on the coals, and brandished the shovel so that the bees were caught in a billowing cloud of smoke. The angry buzzing quieted; the swarm was still. Then, a scented breeze through the open windows caught their attention. As though of one mind, the swarm lifted from Lion and made for the window. Lion stood for a moment as though turned into a pillar of stone and then plummeted to the floor in a dead faint.

Nurse sprang forward. 'Where has he been stung? Oh, Lordy, when he was a boy a bee sting half killed him. His throat all swollen up, and—'

'Fortunately, he was covered with his surplice, but—' Doctor Stewart dropped to his knees beside the patient. 'There are no stings in his face. Check his hands, Tweedie. We must remove any stingers. There are tweezers in my bag.'

Mr Tweedie also knelt. 'Aye, the back of his hands are covered in them. He must have shielded his face with them.' He began to gently remove the tiny, black stingers.

Doctor Stewart laid his ear to Lion's chest, then forced open his mouth. 'Bring me my bag,' he barked at Nurse. His glance went past her to Isabelle, who lay cowering unheeded, on the high, canopied bed. 'And Guisborough, get your wife out of here. Cavendish, help me move him to this table.'

'What are you going to do?' demanded Dominic as he lifted his friend in his arms, disdaining Mr Tweedie's ineffectual assistance.

'His throat has closed up. Nothing for it; I must make a cut, here, in his throat to bypass the swelling.'

'Dear God,' whispered Dominic devoutly.

'Do not be alarmed, it is a perfectly simple procedure,' said Stewart in a reassuring voice. He cast a glance around the room and strode to a small table under the window where a blotter and quill were laid out. He seized the quill and swiftly cut away the ink-stained nib and the feathers, leaving a thin, hollow tube.

'Now, place this cushion under his shoulders and let his head fall back. Tweedie, Cavendish, hold his head and arms—he must not make the slightest movement.'

He rummaged in his bag and brought out an oblong wooden box, which he opened to display a selection of wicked-looking scalpels and forceps. He picked out a thin, flexible hook, which he handed to Mrs Harrison. 'Nurse, be ready to pull back the skin when I make the incision.'

Nurse took her place at Lion's head. Tears ran down her withered cheeks; but her hands were quite steady, and she watched impassively as Stewart made an incision in Lion's distended throat just above the Adam's apple. Doctor Stewart used his fingers to pull back the skin and, with a nod to Nurse, watched as she caught the skin in the hook and held it away from the wound. Then, swiftly and with exceeding skill, the doctor made another, vertical incision in the exposed windpipe. In a few moments, the hollow quill had been inserted into the incision and taped in place. Then the doctor leant forward and gently breathed into the tube. With a sound like a sigh, they saw Lion's chest move.

Dominic became aware of a low, monotonous hum in his ear and realised that Mr Tweedie had been mumbling prayers to himself throughout the procedure. He felt like offering up a prayer himself. 'Will he be all right?' he murmured to the doctor.

'Right as rain. The swelling will subside by and by.' He looked up at Nurse. 'Do you have to hand that concoction you paint on the children's throats?'

'Aye, Sir. I have some in my room.'

'What is in it?'

'Onion, fennel, parsley—you know, Doctor, to bring down the swelling.'

'Yes, all excellent in this case. Bring me some.'

Nurse laid her palm against Lion's cheek. 'I'll be back, my darling boy,' she whispered.

His head moved a little on the cushion, and his lips moved. 'Kate—' It was no more than a breath but Dominic understood. He took Lion's hand in a strong clasp.

'We'll send for her; don't fret old chap. I'm not leaving you until she comes.'

Guisborough came back into the room. 'Poor fellow. He never even finished the prayer. And my wife is more distressed than ever. All for nothing!'

Dominic did not answer. He was turning over the recent events in his mind. How it had been managed he did not know, but that swarm had been deliberately introduced into the chamber. An expression came over his face that a score of hard-bitten ruffians would have recognised—and feared. The murderer had struck too close to home—no one was going to attack a friend of Young Nick's and get away with it!

Nine: If I Were A Bee, Where Would I Be?

'But, my darling idiot, it wasn't supernatural. It was bees!' said Dominic, holding his wife's hand in a comforting clasp.

'I know, but—but why did they attack Lion and only Lion?' Cecily said in a small voice. 'It was as though they were—sent!'

They were alone together in the Earl's library awaiting the arrival of Kate Leonard, and Doctor Carter, who had been summoned from Alford with all dispatch. A youthful and excited groom had carried the message, and it seemed likely that he and his equally young and excitable horse would speedily execute the errand.

Dominic, with all his experience in the Peninsula war and among the Gentlemen, had, nevertheless, taken some time to regain his self-possession after his disagreeable experience. Indeed, he was still rather pale. Cecily, completely overset, sat in a small huddled heap, clutching her husband's hand. 'I blame myself,' she said, weeping softly. 'It was I who wanted to investigate. I thought it would be fun—fun! And now poor Lion is lying there, and who knows if he will—will—oh, Dominic—what if he should die?'

He pulled her close. 'He won't,' he said, with his lips against her hair. 'Stewart knew what he was about, you know. I've seen it done before, on the battlefield, when the fellow standing next to me took a bullet in the mouth' He felt her shudder and lifted a hand to cradle her head against his shoulder.

Cecily recalled Raoul's battlefield story and asked fearfully, 'Did he—that man—live?'

Dominic toyed with the idea of lying to her but, in the end, he shook his head. 'The thing is, darling, that he lay for days in a stinking hospital tent, and the surgeon had enough to do with the other wounded coming in. There was blood and filth all around him, and then he was bundled into an open cart to be taken to the nearest town. So he died from want of care. But Lion has Stewart and Nurse to watch over him—and soon

Kate and dear old Doctor Carter. He'll be right as rain—you'll see.'

They were startled when the door opened suddenly, for they had heard no sounds of approach. Cecily was just reflecting that Kate and Doctor Carter had arrived sooner than appeared possible when Raoul and Abby came hurriedly into the room.

'We were driving into Alford when we met your messenger riding *ventre à terre*. He almost sent us into a ditch, so I demanded of him what he was about—and he told us.'

'Poor Lion,' lamented Abby as she sat beside Cecily and took her hands. 'And poor you. It must have been terrible. I well remember when Lion was stung when we were children.' She turned to Dominic. 'You were away at school, I think, Dom. He lay gasping for breath, and his face grew so fat and swollen. It was horrible.'

'Ah, it is so with those sensitive to the venom,' interposed Raoul. 'Each successive attack produces a stronger reaction.'

'You know about bees?' said Dominic, rather surprised.

'But yes. My father kept bees. It was one of his interests.'

'I wonder if that is why the swarm attacked Lion and none of the rest of us. Do they have some sense of those who are most in danger from them?' said Dominic.

'You mean like cats who inevitably curl up in the lap of the person in the room who detests them most?'

'Well—yes.'

'*Non, mon ami*, they are extremely intelligent, but not—what would you say?—psychic.' He paused and looked thoughtful. 'There are, however, strains of the insect that are vengeful. Have you noticed how, if you swat a bee or wasp, many more will swarm around you?'

'But they went after Lion before—before he had a chance to defend himself.'

'Where is he now?'

'They have put him to bed. Doctor Stewart has said he should not be moved.'

'*Bien*! Bring me then the clothes he was wearing.'

Dominic jumped to his feet and gave a mock salute. '*A la instant, mon Capitain*!'

Cecily occupied the few minutes of his absence relating the account Dominic had given her of the exorcism and its terrible consequences. When he returned, he had, over his arm, Lion's cassock and surplice, together with the shirt and breeches he had worn under them. Raoul turned them over, rather gingerly, and felt delicately in the pockets.

The surplice, shirt, and breeches he discarded. But, when he searched the cassock, he gave a cry of triumph and pulled out the squashed corpse of a very large bee out of the pocket.

'*La Reine*, no less. No wonder they went for him!'

'What the devil? How did that get there?' Dominic walked over to inspect the body. 'His pocket was covered by the surplice. Besides, it's just a slit.'

'The answer, my friend, is that it was put there.'

'Raoul, my love, how did you know to examine Lion's clothes?' asked Abby with a puzzled frown. 'Did you know what you would find?'

'Ah, *ma belle*! Simply, there is a scent released when a bee is killed. That is why the swarm attacked him.'

'A very neat trick,' commented Dominic approvingly. 'It nicely put an end to the exorcism, thus cancelling out any benefit Lady Guisborough might have gained from it, without lessening the atmosphere of fear and superstition. I take my hat off to this villain—he's very inventive.'

'And were not all your suspects most conveniently in the room? Stewart, Tweedie, Guisborough?'

'Well, at least this confirms it must be one of them,' said Dominic. 'No one else could have slipped the queen into Lion's pocket.'

'*Au contraire*. I take it Lion did not drive to Coningsby in full clerical dress?'

'No, of course not. He changed here.'

'And were his vestments packed in a valise?'

'Yes.'

'Was that valise within your sight the entire time?'

'I do not recall—'

'No,' cried Cecily. 'It was not. Lion handed it to the butler. When we reached Isabella's bedchamber, they were laid out on the chaise.'

'So? And I think the so very dignified butler did not himself lay out the clothes. It would be quite beneath him. So a footman—a housemaid—? Someone open to a bribe? Or simply too accustomed to taking orders to question when sent from the room for a moment.'

'So we are back to suspecting everyone in the household again,' said Dominic disgustedly.

'How do you imagine it was done—I mean—the swarm coming out of the fireplace like that?' Cecily was regarding Raoul with awe, as the oracle of all things bee related.

'Oh, that's easy,' interposed Dominic. 'We used to do it when we were children. You take an empty jar in one hand, the lid in the other, and when the bee is busy with a flower, clap the two together around him.'

'Why on earth did you do that?' demanded his wife.

'Oh, we'd shake up the jar, throw it on the ground, and the bees would come out, buzzing with fury, and we'd try to outrun them.'

'Yes, that was how Lion got stung,' said Abby in a reproving voice. 'He couldn't run as fast as you and the other boys.'

'Dash it, don't blame me—I wasn't even there!'

'Yes, but what about the chimney?' interrupted Cecily.

'Well, once he had collected enough bees, he could climb up to the roof and tip the jar—probably a bell-jar—down the chimney. The bees would swarm down the flue and out into the room, where they would scent their dead queen.'

Seeing that his wife looked distinctly sceptical, he suggested they all repair to the roof and investigate. A passing pageboy was suborned to guide them to the roof, which had several points of egress throughout the upper stories of the house. The lad obligingly brought them to the entrance closest to the tower. They stood on the leads regarding the chimney, which stood at least twenty feet higher than themselves. It was designed to resemble a tall, narrow tower with a crenellated crown mimicking that of the tower next to it.

'But it would be madness!' exclaimed Cecily. 'He would have needed a ladder. Surely, the whole county could have seen a man trying to climb a ladder holding an enormous jar in his arms?'

Dominic walked around the tower. 'No, he wouldn't. Look at this.' He pointed to a series of iron rungs set in the brickwork forming a ladder to the top. 'On this side, he's shielded from view by the towers and the other chimney stacks. He could climb up in a couple of minutes, haul the jar up by a rope or some such contrivance, set the bees on their merry way into the flue, and be down again in a few moments.'

'Then it cannot have been any of the three who were in the room when it happened,' cried Cecily in a despairing wail. 'There wasn't time!'

'No, but we have already decided, haven't we, that there is an accomplice?'

'No—wait! It could have been done by one man,' said Abby. 'He could have introduced the bees into the chimney before you were all assembled as long as the damper was down in the hearth. Then, when he was ready, he could have surreptitiously opened it up, and I suppose the light would have attracted them— What do you think, Raoul?'

'What is this—damper? he asked, unfamiliar with the word.

'It shuts off the air flow to the hearth to direct the smoke around the chimney system.'

'Ah, I see. Yes, it could work. The sooty atmosphere in the chimney would calm the bees, but once they found the way out—yes, it could be done.'

'Oh, Lord, every time I think we've cleared someone, it turns out they could have done it anyway,' groaned Dominic.

Cecily was staring at the chimney as though mesmerised. 'Yes, but—there were hundreds of bees. He could not have collected so many between the time we arrived and—and—when it happened.'

'I don't think he did,' answered Dominic. 'I'll wager any money that this effect had been planned for some other use—and a different target. But, when the opportunity presented itself, he could not resist.'

'Ah, yes, we begin to learn something of this villain, do we not?' said Raoul. 'We are looking for a man—'

'Or woman,' put in Abby quickly.

'Or a woman,' her husband agreed smoothly. 'A man or a woman who appears as normal and sane as any of us.'

'A good actor then,' said Dominic.

'The best,' said Raoul with a nod. 'And, like any actor, he enjoys to put on a show for us, with his spectres and his demon bees. But, as well as this, he is the director. We are all his puppets. He likes to pull the strings and watch us dance.'

'To me,' said Dominic in a considering tone, 'that speaks of someone who has very little genuine power in normal life. Someone who has suppressed his natural instincts and breaks out now in these ridiculous gothic effects.'

'It shows some imagination,' said Cecily, musing. 'And a certain warped sense of humour.'

'Not to mention an atrocious taste in fiction,' said Dominic, teasingly. 'I am leaning towards our villain being a female.'

She gave him a pitying smile. 'Very funny, darling. But do be serious. Do you think all this could be done by a woman—really? It seems very farfetched to me.'

He sobered instantly. 'Why not. None of it has needed any very great physical strength. And—if the perpetrator is indeed insane—mad people often do possess superhuman strength.'

Cecily shuddered. 'What a horrible thought.'

He put an arm around her shoulders. 'And that is why, my darling wife, you will leave this investigation to me and Raoul from now on.' He saw her open her lips to protest, and he stopped them with a kiss.

'Very well, Dominic,' said Cecily meekly, as soon as she was able. 'I promise.'

Ten: The Apothecary

The friends had not anywhere near reached an end to their deliberations when they decided to return to Chertsey House for dinner, refusing the Earl's courteous but unenthusiastic invitation to dine with him. Waiting only for the arrival of Kate with the Alford physician, they left Lion, who was recovering well from his ordeal, in their hands and took their departure. It was four o'clock in the afternoon when the Marquis de Saint Michel's curricle swept up to Chertsey House and drew to a halt behind an old-fashioned, one-horse carriage. 'But what is this?' called the Marquis to the butler who came out to greet him. 'Remove me this abominable vehicle!'

'Beg pardon, Sir. It is Mr Newman's gig. We were not expecting you, or I should have had it taken around to the stables, of course.'

'The apothecary! *Qui est-ce qui est malade*? The child?'

'Louis!' cried Abby, preparing to spring from the curricle

'Master Louis is a little bilious, Ma'am. That is all, and nothing to worry you, I'm sure.'

Raoul passed the reins to Dominic, jumped down from the curricle, and handed down his wife. They dashed impetuously into the house. Both the butler and Dominic regarded the retreating backs in some surprise. They exchanged a glance that seemed to say 'French!'

The butler turned to ascend the steps. Just as he did so, a fussy little gentleman of perhaps fifty years appeared in the doorway. His shovel hat and leather case informed Dominic that this must be the apothecary. And the apothecary was one of their suspects—one whom they had completely forgotten to interview.

'Might I have a word with you, Mr Newman!' he called, backing the horses a little. 'I have been wanting to consult you. If you can spare me some time now, there will be no need for you to visit my grandmother's house.'

'Your grandmother, Sir?'

'The Dowager Lady Cavendish.'

The little man bowed. 'I am honoured, Sir. I may say I knew your father, and you have a great look of him, a very great look of him.'

Dominic, perceiving that a groom had come around the corner of the house, sprang down from the box of the curricle, and assisted Cecily to descend. He noticed the apothecary's wistful gaze on the two beautifully matched bays and smiled. 'You are a judge of horseflesh, Mr Newman?'

'I am, Sir. You might say I grew up with horses. My grandfather was a farrier.'

'Indeed? When I was a boy, my father's farrier was my best friend.'

Mr Newman sighed. 'I should have liked to follow in his footsteps. But my father thought it low, and so, instead, I took up *his* occupation and became an apothecary.'

Friendly relations having been established, Dominic proceeded to consult Mr Newman about some wholly imaginary symptoms. That gentleman said that he would send up a draught that would infallibly alleviate the pangs of indigestion. 'Though I would suggest, Sir, if you will forgive the impertinence, a bottle or two less with dinner might prove just as efficacious.'

'Exactly what I said,' interposed Cecily in a very wifely manner.

'I shall bear it in mind,' promised Dominic, with his charming smile. 'This was a fortunate chance—our meeting like this—I mean. The Earl was saying only the other day how much he relies on your services.'

'You refer, Sir, to Lord Guisborough?'

'Alas, yes. You and your son have attended Lady Guisborough, along with Doctor Stewart, I believe.'

'I have indeed, my Lord, but not my son. He can't face going to the Park—not now.'

'He cannot face it?' repeated Dominic. 'Now, why is that?'

'He has had a blow. A severe blow.'

Dominic said nothing but looked all interest. Mr Newman continued. 'You will have heard, perhaps, of the explosion at the pit on his Lordship's property?'

'Yes, he told me of it himself.'

'Well, my boy was courting the daughter of the pit foreman, a very nice girl. She was taking her father a bite of dinner when it happened.'

'Good God! Was she hurt?'

'Dead, Sir. They couldn't find enough of her to bury,' answered the apothecary shaking his head.

'What a tragedy!' said Cecily with sincerest sympathy.

'And what a motive for murder,' Dominic added to himself. Aloud, he said, 'Does he blame Guisborough, then?'

'Well, my Lord, boys are kittle-cattle, as they say. He knows the Earl is a good man, really. I don't pay any attention to his—' He broke off suddenly, perhaps remembering to whom he spoke.

'His—what, Sir?'

'His nonsensical talk. He wouldn't hurt a fly—not really.' Mr Newman heaved a deeply despondent sigh. 'It is such a pity, Sir. For he used to be in and out of the Park all day when he was a boy.'

Dominic's head was lifted in sudden attention. 'Oh? Knows the place well, does he?'

Mr Newman nodded. 'Every nook and cranny. You see, the wife's brother is head groom up at the Park. Sammy used to help him in the stables and pretty much had the run of the house, such a favourite he was with the upper servants, so full of fun and gig! And they had him in at Christmas to sing for poor Lady Guisborough that was the Earl's first wife. She would say he sang like an angel. And when they dressed him up like an angel, he looked the part. He did, indeed. He favours his mother, you see, Sir. She was thought a great beauty when I married her. Pretty as a picture, both of them, with their golden hair and blue eyes.'

He hesitated and cleared his throat. 'I'm very glad I ran into you, Sir. Very glad. That boy of mine has got himself into a lot of trouble with his wild talk about getting back at his Lordship. Now I've heard rumours about that business over at Alford, and how you cleared it up. If you would condescend to have a word with Sammy—make him see he's doing himself no good—I would be very much obliged to you.'

Dominic could not see why the boy should pay the slightest heed to anyone so unconnected with him, but as he wished very much to interview him and had not known how to suggest it himself, he readily acquiesced. It was agreed that Mr Newman should bring his son to see Sir Dominic the following day, and the two men parted with mutual expressions of esteem.

During the sumptuous—and very Gallic—dinner of Abby's providing, the conversation was confined to general subjects. No one had the slightest doubt that the servants were as well aware of what was going on at the Park as their employers were, but the proprieties must be maintained.

The gentlemen did not linger over their port and very soon joined the ladies in the drawing room. They found them sipping tea and waiting, in some impatience, for their husbands' entrance.

'What an age you have been,' said Cecily, rather crossly.

'We were drinking your health, darling,' he answered, taking the seat next to her on the sofa and putting an arm around her shoulders. 'And Abby's, too, of course.'

'Well, now you are here—'

'What we need now,' said Dominic, 'is a review of what we know for certain and then a plan of campaign to find the perpetrator. We are in a far better position than before because we know that it has to be someone who has a right to be at the Park, at least some of the time, and who knows it well.'

'And he must have an accomplice—a woman—a fair woman—who could lure poor Isabella out of her chamber,' Cecily reminded him.

'She need not be fair,' objected Abby. 'She could wear a wig.'

'She need not even be a "she" at all,' interposed Raoul. 'In her drugged state, Lady Guisborough could be deceived by a man in a wig and gown, if he were *un jeune homme mince*—young and—what is the word?—slender.'

'And now we know that whoever it may be understands all about bees,' interpolated Abby.

'Far, far more people than I ever dreamed of seem to be experts,' complained Cecily. 'Even Raoul.'

Dominic brushed this aside. 'In any event,' he said, 'I do not believe that these are the acts of a madman. But what do you all think?'

'I am not sure I can agree with you there,' said Raoul, with a grimace. 'There is planning and intelligence here, certainly. But we must not forget a madman can act sane enough when the frenzy is not upon him.'

'Well, let us review our list of "possibles" in light of what we have learnt.' He leant back against the back of the sofa and stretched his legs. 'Will you take notes, Cecily?'

The look she cast him would have abashed a far more dictatorial husband than Dominic. 'Oh, very well, give me a tablet then.' Having been supplied with paper and pencil, he proceeded to draw a line down the centre of the page. On the left hand side, he wrote "Name" and, on the other, "Suspicious Circumstances." He then proceeded to list five names, leaving a few lines in the opposing column for each. The names were: Lord Guisborough, Reverend Tweedie, Doctor Stewart, Mr Newman, Samuel Newman, and, upon reflection, he added 'Unknown.'

'You have put Guisborough first, *mon ami*,' noted Raoul. 'You have reason. It is seen that the man with the most desire to be rid of a woman is always the husband.' He caught sight of his wife's indignant face and said soothingly, 'Be easy, ma *Belle*, I have no desire to be rid of you.'

Cecily said in a considering tone, 'Miss Proudie has

always been quite sure the Earl is behind the crimes. But why? Now that I have met him and seen how he adores Isabella, I can think of no reason unless he really is mad. As you said, Dominic, she is not an heiress; he gains nothing from her death.'

'Nevertheless, there are some suspicious circumstances. Firstly, of course, he is on the spot, free to wander wherever he wishes through the house.'

'If it were he, it is odd that he claims not to believe in the ghost,' mused Cecily. 'Surely, whoever it is *wants* people to think Isabella is being haunted.'

'Or that she is mad.'

'But, then, what about the first wife? They cannot both be mad.'

'True,' said Dominic. 'A haunting is a better presumption for the murderer. It keeps the household from being too observant.'

'But again—why?' she demanded in an exasperated tone.

'Ah—when we know that—the mystery explains itself,' remarked Raoul, nodding.

'Well, I think Guisborough is most unlikely to be the culprit,' said Cecily decidedly. 'For one thing, there is no indication that he has ever had any interest in bees. And besides—he loves her—and I believe he loved Caroline. Poor man, my heart bled for him when I saw his face as he bent over Isabella.'

Raoul smiled and raised one eyebrow, 'He is attractive to women, this Earl. It is often so with murderers.'

'Good heavens, if all you have against him is that he is attractive to women, what about the doctor? He is quite *beautiful*!'

Dominic regarded his wife with disfavour. 'Do you think so? You never mentioned it before.' He poised his pencil over the tablet. 'In that case, I'm quite happy to make a case against him.'

'There is no case. Well—apart from those stupid bees.

And we must not forget he saved Lion.' said Cecily. 'Unless there are circumstances we know nothing about, he can have no reason to harm the Guisboroughs for he depends upon their patronage. Perhaps if we knew more about him?'

'If there is anything discreditable in his past, there will be gossip. Presumably, he has a housekeeper—butler—we could make discreet enquiries, perhaps?'

'His sister keeps house for him. He told me so when he visited me.'

Dominic smiled at her. 'There is a nice, safe job for you, my precious one. It would be only polite for you to call upon the doctor's sister while you are in the neighbourhood.'

'But, darling,' said Cecily on an acid note, 'you said yourself that you have to fight women off with a stick. Perhaps you should be the one to question her.'

Dominic allowed a smirk to twist his mouth. 'I might at that. Is she pretty?'

Cecily, annoyed with him for calling her bluff, sent him a dagger glance. 'No, I will do it.'

'Spoilsport,' he said teasingly. 'Of course, the doctor has always been the favourite because he has the best chance to tamper with her medicines. But, again, we come back to *why*.' He noted down "opportunity" in the second column and added a large question mark.

'We seem to have skipped Mr Tweedie,' he remarked. 'But, as far as I can see, we do not have anything against him?'

'There was something—don't you remember? Something about why he had to leave India so suddenly. Perhaps he has some disgraceful secret and is being blackmailed by—'

'By Guisborough? Really, my dear girl, use your brains. Why should the wealthiest man in England blackmail a humble vicar?'

Cecily surveyed him with hostility. 'I was not going to say that at all. I only thought that perhaps he was being used as a catspaw by the real villain.'

'It is not a bad idea, that,' remarked Raoul. 'It is well

imagined.'

Dominic duly noted "Reason – possible blackmail" in the second column. That seemed to dispose of the reverend gentleman.

'Now, for Mr Newman—or, rather, his son,' said Dominic, turning to Raoul. 'We have some new, and very interesting, information. When I first asked Guisborough if anyone might have a grudge against him, he mentioned an explosion at a coal mine he owns in Nottinghamshire. Now it turns out that Sam Newman's sweetheart was killed in the blast. And, if that is not enough to make a man seek revenge, I don't know what is.'

'Oh, the poor young man!' exclaimed Abby, her newly maternal heart moved.

'Oh, oh, oh!' exclaimed Cecily, practically jumping up and down in her seat.

'Having a fit, darling?' enquired Dominic, surveying her in some amusement.

She ignored him and addressed Raoul, who seemed more appreciative of her ideas. 'How if the sweetheart is *not* dead, and the two of them are in it together to be revenged for her father's death?'

Dominic gave a shout of laughter, but Saint Michel paid her the compliment of giving the suggestion his serious consideration. 'Certainly, two young people could play these tricks on the lady, but it is difficult to see how they could introduce the drug into her food. And, if the young man is involved, it would appear the first Lady Guisborough's death was indeed an accident.'

Abby interposed, 'Is it perhaps the case that the two things are separate?'

They stared at her, struck by the thought. 'You mean that the tricks and the poisoning are perpetrated by different individuals? Surely that is too much of a coincidence,' said Dominic slowly.

'It might not be a coincidence at all. The tricks might have been seized on by the poisoner—to shift the blame and confuse the issue.'

'But did not Caroline also see the face in the mirror?' said Cecily. 'I cannot recall what Doctor Stewart said.' She thought for a moment, and then her face lit up. 'I remember now! He said Caroline heard sobbing and thought it was the ghost of the cavalier lady whose husband was killed at—at—wherever it was. But he was certain she did not *see* anything.'

Dominic was busy writing on his tablet. 'I'll bracket Newman and his son together because otherwise the father doesn't come into it at all.' He looked up and said with a rueful smile, 'Which just leaves us with "Unknown."'

'It cannot be "Unknown,"' objected Cecily. 'We know it has to be someone familiar with the Park, and permitted to go about it as they wish. So, unless we suspect servants who have been with the family for thirty years or more—'

'Not all of them. What about the lady's maid?'

'I had forgotten all about her,' admitted Cecily. 'Of course one does not meet the lady's maid when one calls in the normal way, but under the circumstances— Where was she during all the commotion today?'

'I can think of a dozen reasons why she might have been absent,' said Dominic with odious complacency. 'She may have gone into Lincoln to collect a package for her mistress at the Receiving Office, or purchase some ribbon or lace or any of the fallals women can't live without.'

Cecily did not dignify this with an answer. But Raoul said, with a twist of his humorous mouth, 'There are other attractions in Lincoln, *mon ami*, for an enterprising young lady.'

'Such as?' asked Cecily, still glowering at her husband.

'Officers, *Cherie*. Many, many bored young officers, far from home and in need of—diversion.'

'Men!' exclaimed Abby in a disgusted voice. 'I will have you know that women think far less about you than you do about yourselves.'

He grinned at her. 'Do you care to make a wager, my adored one?'

Abby, possibly softened by this mode of address, declined to do so. 'But that does not mean I agree with your maligning a perfectly unknown young female.'

Raoul—who had, unbeknown to his lady, visited a hostelry in Lincoln a few nights earlier and made the acquaintance of Marie-Claire—held his peace.

Eleven: Lady Cavendish and the Doctor's Sister

It was at two-o'clock the following afternoon when the Dowager's barouche drew up in front of the doctor's house. It was a modern villa, neat and pretty, with all the elegances of white stucco, wrought-iron balconies, and bow windows, charmingly set within a flower-filled garden. The vision of the good doctor as their sinister villain retreated still further.

Cecily had pictured the doctor's sister as a frail, middle-aged lady, perhaps wrapped in shawls against the unseasonable summer chill. She was therefore quite unprepared when the elderly parlour maid who answered the door ushered her into a sunny room overlooking the back lawn and inhabited by a girl who appeared to be no more than eighteen years old. She was quite as pretty as her brother was handsome. She had the same golden curls and blue eyes but was blessed with the additional charms of creamy skin, a straight little nose, and a soft, rosebud mouth.

Cecily gave a startled exclamation, then blushed and said apologetically, 'Are you Miss Stewart? Pray forgive me. When the doctor told me his sister kept house for him, I had expected to be introduced to a much older lady.'

The girl smiled and came forward, saying in a soft, appealing voice, 'People are quite often surprised. But my parents had long given up any thought of adding to their family when I came along. There are fifteen years between me and Hector, and ten more between my eldest brother and him.' She shook hands with Cecily and gestured to a chair by the open windows that led onto a paved terrace. 'If it is not too cold for you, I like to sit here and enjoy the fresh air.'

'Thank you, this is delightful.' Cecily settled herself in a Windsor chair and gazed admiringly at the view across the smooth green lawn, the little wood, and, beyond, a shining gleam of water meandering through its own little valley. 'Why, are those not the towers of Coningsby Park over there beyond the river? I did not know we were so close.'

'It is not as close as it appears. About two miles as the

crow flies, but all of five miles by road.' Miss Stewart followed the direction of Cecily's gaze. 'I always think it looks like an enchanted castle,' she added dreamily. 'Do you not think so?'

Cecily smiled. 'Yes, from here. But, close up, it seems to me a dark, uncomfortable place. This house is so much pleasanter.'

Miss Stewart appeared shocked. 'Oh, how can you compare the two? The one so full of history and character, while this is so—so—commonplace.'

'There is a little too much character for my poor friend Isabella,' answered Cecily rather tartly.

'Oh?' Miss Stewart appeared to be uninterested. 'She has nervous fancies, so my brother says.' She folded her hands in her lap and said rather contemptuously, 'She should concern herself with her husband and her household. She would soon recover from these nonsensical ideas.'

It was apparent to Cecily that Doctor Stewart had kept his sister in ignorance of the true state of affairs at the Park. Yet it was strange that she had not heard the story elsewhere—in the village or out in the wider parish. Did the child meet no one? She set herself to find out. 'Have you been in the district long? I have many friends here, especially around Alford, but I do not think they have the pleasure of your acquaintance. Your brother, of course, is well known and universally respected.'

'I have been here six years,' the girl answered in her gentle way.

'Why, then, you must know Lion and Kate Leonard, the Fanshawe family—' her voice trailed off as the other girl shook her golden curls. 'What, you do not visit—anywhere?'

'No, nowhere,' was the reply.

'But, you have visitors?'

Again the shake of the head. 'You are the first caller I have had. Except for Lord Guisborough, of course. He came often—before.'

'Before—?'

'His marriage.'

'I see.'

'Before he met her—he seemed to like me,' her voice trembled a little. 'Then he went away to Lincoln and, when he returned, he was different.' The soft, childish lips quivered. 'Then he liked her best.'

'You are fond of Lord Guisborough?'

'He is the handsomest, most charming, kindest, and best man I have ever known,' came the response. Cecily shot her a sudden, questioning look. There had been something odd about her tone. It was almost as though she answered by rote, like an obedient child repeating a lesson. And surely, even a shy girl who had met no other men could not really think him handsome, or his odd manners charming. But, then, she had known him a long time, presumably, and, after all, Isabella had grown to love him. 'He is most amiable,' she acknowledged. 'I am sorry if his marriage distressed you.'

She half expected her hostess to respond angrily, for the remark was certainly impertinent. But the only answer was a sigh. Then, quite suddenly, she stiffened, her eyes widened, and a lovely blush suffused her cheeks. Cecily glanced across the lawn to see what had aroused her interest. She beheld a young man on horseback trotting smartly along a lane that, previously hidden from view, skirted the doctor's garden. He caught sight of the girl in the window, and his eyes glowed with a quite unmistakeable ardour. Then he became aware of Cecily seated beside her and, in an instant, had schooled his expression to one of impersonal courtesy. He doffed his hat. 'Good day, Miss Stewart,' he called in a clear, cheery voice.

'Good Day, Mr Repton.' Cecily glanced at the girl, puzzled. Her voice was startlingly different from the strange, subdued tone she had used when she talked about Lord Guisborough. There was real interest, real animation in her voice and face now.

'What a handsome young man,' she said, watching the

other girl's face as the young man rode on. 'How did you become acquainted? Did your brother introduce him to you?'

'Oh no!' She looked almost frightened at the thought. 'Hector would not like me to—the family are *manufacturers*, you see.' She spoke as though announcing that the Reptons were well-known criminals. 'Hector does not know about— does not know—you will not tell him?' she finished in an anxious tone.

'Certainly not, if you do not wish it. But do, please, satisfy my curiosity. How did you meet, confined as you are?'

The girl blushed rosily once more. 'I was walking in the garden, at dusk. Hector was at the Park, and I felt restless and a little—lonely. All at once, I heard a horrid sound—a squeal of pain—coming from the bluebell wood yonder.' She gestured to the clump of trees beyond the lawn. 'I went through the wicket gate and followed the sound. After a few moments, I found a dear little rabbit, caught in a cruel snare.'

'Oh, poor thing! Was it badly hurt?'

'I think—only when it struggled. There was a wire around its neck, you see. Well, I heard a horse coming along the lane and ran out, and—it was—Mr Repton!'

'And he rescued the rabbit?'

'Oh, yes. He said that it must be the work of a poacher and he would report the matter to his father who is a justice of the peace. I was so very grateful.'

Cecily smiled. 'And since then, have you wandered very often in the bluebell wood at dusk?'

There was so much sympathy and warmth in her smile that the girl's eyes fell, and she admitted, with a shy little laugh, 'Once or twice.'

At that moment, a maidservant appeared, bearing the tea tray. Cecily was a little surprised by the massive silver teapot and milk jug and the dainty china tea service. She had not thought the doctor to be in such affluent circumstances. Miss Stewart poured the tea and pressed Cecily to take a wafer-thin slice of bread and butter.

There was a little stir outside the house, the front door was opened and closed, and Doctor Stewart entered the room. It would have been too much to say that his sister looked frightened, but the bright eyes dimmed a little and the happy, girlish little smile vanished. 'Oh, Hector, do see who has come to call upon me.'

But he had already seen Cecily and was bowing before her. 'Lady Cavendish! How very kind of you to visit Alana.'

'Alana? What a lovely name! Is it Scottish?'

'Aye, Gaelic. It means "beautiful."' He continued teasingly, 'My mother tells me she was a beautiful baby—I dinna ken what went agley.'

Alana laughed, but it did not seem to Cecily a very natural laugh. She thought the girl was a little afraid of her brother. But, after all, the doctor was much older and stood in the place of a father to her. There was nothing much to be read into that. She filled the little silence that followed by saying, 'Indeed, there is nothing agley—by which, I conjecture, you mean amiss—for your sister—may I call you Alana?—is quite the prettiest girl I have seen in this part of the country.'

'Until you came,' responded Doctor Stewart gallantly.

'Oh, I do not count myself a girl, but an old married lady. And, even if I were not, I am quite eclipsed by your sister's lovely golden curls. Just like a princess in some old fable.'

'But you are like a princess, too, for some have hair as "black as ebony" remember,' interpolated Alana shyly.

'Do you know, I do not think I should like to be a princess at all,' answered Cecily with a merry smile. 'Only, think how uncomfortable, having to battle with dragons and witches and wicked stepmothers! And, in real life, could one count on a handsome prince to rescue one?'

'But can you doubt it?' said the doctor. 'You would be overwhelmed with princes, I dare say.'

Alana picked up a rose-painted pot and said, 'Would you like a little honey with your bread, dear Lady Cavendish? It is from our own bees.'

Doctor Stewart bent forward and plucked the pot out of her hand. 'I'm sure Lady Cavendish would prefer some of our damson jam, which I see on the tray. Will you not try some, Ma'am? Our good Mrs Bundy uses some secret ingredient—I rather suspect she purloins my port—but the result is excellent.'

Cecily politely accepted the spoonful of deep-red preserve that he placed on her plate and spread some upon her bread. She did not need to feign appreciation. 'Oh, this is quite the most delicious damson jam I have tasted!'

Doctor Stewart looked gratified. 'I shall ask Mrs Bundy to send a half-dozen jars over to Maythorpe with my compliments.'

Cecily thanked him with real gratitude. 'How very kind.' Then, turning back to her hostess, she remarked, 'Doctor Stewart has been telling me how very keen he is on his beekeeping.'

The doctor answered before Alana could speak. 'Aye, and m'sister, too. She has a way with the bees, and I swear they like her the better of us two. I have been stung many times, but she—never.'

Cecily turned to Alana in lively surprise. 'Truly? How very brave of you. I should not dare approach them. One of our neighbours in Hertfordshire kept bees, and I would always run past the hives as fast as I could when we were obliged to go that way.'

'Oh, there is no danger, if you know what you are about,' said Alana in a soft voice, blushing a little.

'Well, I think you are quite wonderful. Especially after what happened yesterday to my poor friend. Indeed now, I am quite terrified of the horrid creatures.'

The girl gave her a quick, sidelong glance. 'Yes, Hector told me. It was very unfortunate. But really, they rarely attack. I cannot think how it happened.'

'That is just as well. Of course, Lion is particularly sensitive to the venom, so I am told. The consequences would not have been so—so—calamitous, had it not been so.'

Then, as she fancied she saw a weariness upon her young hostess' face, she stood and shook out her skirts. 'This has been a delightful visit, but I believe I must go home. My own "prince" will be wanting his dinner very soon.' She took Alana's hand and, then, on impulse, kissed her cheek. 'May I come again?'

The girl shot a quick look at her brother and then said, with the colour once more suffusing her cheeks, 'Thank you, I should like that very much.'

Doctor Stewart escorted Cecily to the barouche and handed her into it with a gallant air. 'Thank you for visiting the child. It has done her good. I wish I could prevail upon her to go about more.'

'Oh? I got the impression—' she broke off, aware that she had been about to be indiscreet.

'That it was I who disapproved of her making new acquaintances?'

'Well, yes.'

'Not at all, but I have never been able to interest her in any acquaintance but one. She was very much—attached—to my friend Guisborough, and when he ceased to come to the house—well, she retreated into herself.'

Cecily pondered this on the way home, and when she recounted the conversation to Dominic over dinner, she said, 'I don't believe Hector Stewart knows the first thing about his sister. She is shy, certainly, but she seemed to be very pleased to see me, and there is no doubt she has been meeting young Repton on the sly.'

He inspected the dish in front of him and was pleased to approve. Through a mouthful of fried whitebait, he said, 'Do you think she is in love with Guisborough?'

Cecily shook her head decidedly. 'I saw her face when Mr Repton rode by. It is he she loves. But I think she had a childish sort of worship for the Earl, fostered, I think, by her brother, who encouraged him to call.'

'You think he was doing a spot of matchmaking?'

'Well, you cannot blame him. Any man would wish his sister to become a countess.'

'Very true. Although, given Guisborough's history, being his wife seems to be fraught with danger.' He lifted his head, listening. 'Now who can that be?'

'What? Who?'

'I hear horses upon the drive. It is a little late for visitors.'

Cecily clasped her hands together. 'I pray it is not bad news of Lion.'

Presently, there was a rather tentative rap upon the door knocker, and they heard Fothergill's stately tread as he went unhurriedly to answer it. There was a murmured conversation, and then the butler entered the room and said with austere disapproval, 'Mr Newman and Mr Samuel Newman are awaiting you in the morning room, Sir. As I was not aware that you had sent for the apothecary, I told Mr Newman I would enquire if you were at home.'

'Good Lord! I had forgotten all about Newman.' He tossed down his napkin and made as though to leave the table.

'Dominic, you have had a mere mouthful of dinner. Surely, Mr Newman will not object to wait until—'

'Oh, this will not take long. Send a message to the kitchens, Fothergill, if you please. Delay the next course by half an hour or so.'

'Very good, Sir.' He held open the door for Dominic to pass through and, in the process, exchanged a speaking glance with Cecily. 'A very impulsive gentleman, Sir Dominic,' he permitted himself to remark. 'Always was—from a boy.'

However, that impulsive gentleman entered the morning room with the grave and magisterial air of a grandfather. He had been asked by the father to remonstrate with the young man, and he had every intention of doing so—while carrying out a little investigative work on his own account.

He was rather taken aback when introduced to the lad by his anxious father. Mr Newman had described his son when a child as 'pretty as a picture.' He was still a pretty youth, angelically fair, with wide-set, light-blue eyes and a complexion any young lady might envy. There was scarcely a hair upon his rounded chin, and he showed a tendency to blush whenever Dominic addressed him. He certainly did not look like the kind of fire-eater to threaten violence and mayhem.

'Will you not take a seat, Mr Newman?' Dominic said with his attractive smile.

'I'd rather stand, thank you, Sir.' He pushed his son forward. 'Sammy, you listen to what Sir Dominic has to say to you and take heed.'

Sammy muttered something inaudible and hung his head. 'Speak up,' adjured his father.

'I said I don't care what no one says,' uttered the boy in a goaded voice.

Before the apothecary could speak, Dominic said kindly, 'I understand you have recently lost your sweetheart in tragic circumstances. I offer you my deepest condolences.'

The boy's cheek grew crimson. 'Thank you.'

'Thank you—*Sir*,' interpolated his father.

Dominic moved to the fireplace and took up a position with one arm stretched along the mantle. He stared down into the flames. 'I can imagine—I am myself newly married, and there was a time when my wife was in danger. One would go to any lengths to protect—or avenge—the lady one loved.'

Both father and son stared at him. Obviously, this was not what they had expected to hear. He smiled rather ruefully. 'But you know, the danger to my wife came from quite another source than I had anticipated. It was, in fact, pure chance that I was able to thwart her attacker. Are you so very sure, Mr Samuel, that the Earl is to blame for what happened?'

'T'was his workings, an' he was warned of the danger.'

'I know. He told me himself that he had wished to close the mine but was persuaded to keep it open because the men needed the work and the danger was slight. He is no engineer, and so he took advice from those he thought more knowledgeable than himself. And then, you know, he had to make a choice between the very slight possibility of an explosion and the certain disaster of unemployment among the colliers' families. What would you have done?'

The boy's big eyes grew moist. 'It may be as you say, Sir. But it don't bring Susan back.'

'No—I know. But would she have wanted you to risk gaol, perhaps even transportation? To be making threats against a man in the Earl's position is not wise. He is a member of the government—it might be called sedition.'

'There Sammy! What did I tell you?' said his father in the tone of one who has been proved justified.

'And you know, the Earl has trouble of his own. His wife is very unwell. You would not wish to add to the family's distress, would you?'

Sammy shook his head. 'I got nothing against her ladyship. She is a sweet lady—too good for him!'

'I think you knew his first wife, too. Your father tells me she would have you in at Christmas to sing to her.'

For the first time, the boy smiled. 'Aye, that she did. She was very kind to me, always.' He added simply, 'I loved her.'

Dominic had a sudden inspiration. 'Then it is you who keeps the urn in the crypt full of fresh flowers?'

The boy's eyes fell, and he blushed. 'Everyone but me seems to have forgotten her. Poor lady.'

'You know there is an absurd rumour that her ghost walks—and that the new Lady Guisborough is driven almost to madness by her visitations?'

The youth looked quite astonished. Dominic reflected that he was either a surpassingly good actor, or he had really heard nothing of the dark happenings at Coningsby Park. 'No, Sir, I ain't heard anything 'bout that. Why it's a faradiddle! She wouldn't have hurt a fly when she was alive—why should she now?'

'A very good point. It must have been a happy household,' he continued, 'with such a kind lady as mistress.

104

I believe the Earl was devoted to her.'

'I dunno about that,' muttered Sammy. 'He don't show much.'

'No, that is not his way. Did her ladyship seem fond of him?'

'Thought the sun shone—' he broke off, catching his father's eye.

'Indeed? Then, for her sake, will you not forget these foolish thoughts of revenge? You will not injure the Earl, you know, but you may do yourself a great deal of harm.'

Sammy lifted his face, and Dominic saw that the blue eyes were swimming with tears. 'If you had seen Susan, Sir. She was so young, and pretty, and a bit heedless. She hadn't done nothing to deserve what happened to her.'

Dominic was moved by the boy's simple words. He stepped forward and placed a hand upon Sammy's shoulder. 'I know, believe me, I know. I lost a most beloved sister, far, far too young. But, in time, your grief will fade and you will be happy again.'

'I'll not forget her!'

'No, of course not. Let her memory be a guide in everything you do. But you must let go of your hatred first. Do not let it consume you.'

'I'll try, Sir,' said the boy, wiping his eyes with the back of his hand. 'And, thank you. I didn't know you'd be so kind.'

Dominic suffered a twinge of conscience. He had been genuinely sympathetic, but the back of his mind had been busy with his investigation. Still, he was now fairly sure that they could dismiss any suspicions of Sammy Newman—or of his father—which was a satisfactory end to the interview.

Twelve: Enter the Heir

'Do you care to accompany me into Lincoln today?' asked Dominic the next morning as he pushed away his breakfast plate.

'Lincoln? Yes, of course, but what have you to do there?'

'I need to have a word with old Colonel Crowther. The excise officers have become devilish slack about patrols. I think a little military discipline is in order.'

'Patrols? Oh, you mean against the Gentlemen.' She looked a little reproachful. 'Do you really want to have your old shipmates incarcerated in Lincoln Gaol?'

'Aye, and hanged, too! Don't fall into the trap of thinking that the free traders are romantic. They are a parcel of murderous cutthroats, I can tell you.'

'You were romantic,' she said with a saucy smile.

'Well, I was not the genuine article.'

'And Raoul was romantic. I suppose you would say he was not the genuine article, either.'

'Exactly. He was merely a French spy, and he played a dishonourable game—honourably. But these fellows—why, just last month, a revenue man disappeared in Skegness. He was on his way to the Vine to arrest old Tom Hewson and hasn't been seen since. I think I can guess what happened to him, and I doubt if he died quickly, poor fellow.'

'Ugh! Don't Dominic.' She shuddered and clutched his hand.

'I'm sorry, darling—don't worry your head about it. I'm not involved with smugglers anymore—only slavers.'

She looked up at him with shining eyes. 'Dominic, if there must be such evil people in the world, I am very glad that you are leading in the fight against them.'

He clasped her hand and bent to kiss her cheek. 'That's my girl! What will you do in Lincoln while I am at the garrison?'

'Oh, I have a few purchases to make and I will call in at the receiving office to see if a package I ordered from London has arrived.'

'A package? You are very mysterious. Aren't you going to tell me what is in it?'

'No.'

'Very well, I shall contain my soul in patience. Shall you be ready in half-an-hour?'

'Certainly, I have only to change my gown and put on my bonnet.'

'I'll order the carriage to come round in a couple of hours then.'

She cuffed him playfully. 'Half-an-hour will be perfectly adequate, thank you.'

It was rather more than half-an-hour, but considerably within the two hours, that the chaise set off. Had Dominic been alone he would have preferred to ride, but as his wife accompanied him, he had elected to convey her in the comfort of his grandmother's coach. A smart groom rode at the rear of the coach, and would perform the functions of a footman, escorting Cecily around the town and carrying her inevitable parcels.

'I cannot conceive why I should need an escort,' she had objected. 'Surely, no harm can come to me in the centre of the town.'

'You will do as you are told, for once,' her husband answered sternly. 'What with the assizes and the militia, not to mention a flood of infantrymen lately turned-off, Lincoln is not the place for a lady to walk alone.'

Cecily acquiesced and was, indeed, quite grateful for the groom's presence once she had seen with her own eyes that Dominic's description of the town centre had been by no means exaggerated. She visited a linen draper, a millinery establishment, and a tea emporium in quick succession and had accumulated quite a number of packages when she suddenly remembered that she had intended to visit the Receiving Office. She smiled at the groom in a confiding manner that made him her slave, as well as her servant, and said, 'Thomas, I am quite lost. Do you know where the Receiving Office may be?'

'Aye, Ma'am, it's none so far. Just down this street and to the left.'

'Thank you. Do you know, I am quite tired of all the crowds and the jostling. I think I shall wait for you inside, if you would go back to the hotel and ask Humphrey to collect me in the chaise.'

'Very good, Ma'am. But I'll just see you safe inside first.'

'You do take good care of me. I shall tell Sir Dominic so.'

The young man blushed. 'Beggin' your pardon, Ma'am, but it's a pleasure to serve a lady like you.'

She was touched. 'Why, thank you, Thomas. Ah, here we are. I shall collect my package and wait for you on that bench against the wall.'

Thomas, having cast a look around to ensure no undesirables were hanging about in the crowd, departed on his errand, while Cecily took her place in the queue at the nearest counter. There were several other queues; and, as usual, she found she had chosen the one that moved the slowest. She amused herself with watching the crowd around her and wondering what could be in some of the strangely shaped packages, or why a particular letter should have made a young woman blush fiery red, or a young man grow pale.

She had noticed a little family group going down the adjacent queue. They were a remarkably handsome couple with a very fine little boy at their side. They reached the counter before she did, and she heard the gentleman say in a clear, well-bred voice, 'Have you any letters for Sullivan, Major Sullivan?'

The name was familiar to Cecily. Surely, she had heard it or read about it, only a few days earlier. Apparently, there was no letter. She heard the gentleman say in a consolatory voice, 'Never fret my dear Maria. It is bound to come soon. Your cousin may be from home, or—'

'Or he does not wish to acknowledge us,' said the lady in

a low voice. 'I did not think Edward would be so unfeeling.'

'Now, my love, a man like Guisborough has many calls upon his time,' answered her husband in a reasonable tone. 'Do not be cast down.'

But the lady covered her face with her hands, and a sob shook her shoulders. The little boy pulled at her elbow crying, 'Mama, Mama, don't cry, don't cry.' Then his own lips began to tremble, and he looked up at his father helplessly. 'What is wrong with Mama?'

Cecily stepped out of the queue and walked boldly up to the gentleman. 'Forgive me, if I am impertinent, but I think perhaps the lady is overcome by the heat. It is horridly close and stuffy in here. My carriage will be at the door directly. Pray allow me to convey you to your home, or hotel, or wherever you wish.'

'You are very kind, Ma'am, but—'

She did not allow him to finish. 'You see, I could not help but hear you mention Guisborough. You must know that Lady Guisborough is an intimate friend. I am sure she would wish me to give you any assistance in my power.'

Sullivan's face cleared. 'You know the Guisboroughs? This is an amazing chance indeed! We will be very happy to accept your offer. May I know to whom I am indebted?'

'I am Lady Cavendish. And who is this young gentleman,' she asked, smiling at the little boy.

'This is my son, Michael,' said Major Sullivan. 'Make your bow to Lady Cavendish, my boy.'

'I am very happy to make your acquaintance, Sir,' Cecily said, stooping gracefully to take the little boy's hands between her own. 'You are just the same age as my own little nephew.'

'What's his name?' asked the child looking up at her with big, solemn eyes.

'His name is Bobby. Perhaps I may introduce you to him. Do you like to play cricket?'

Major Sullivan interposed. 'Michael is not quite well enough to play games at the moment. That is one reason why we wish to—to—consult my wife's cousin.'

'Oh, what a shame!' Cecily noticed the queue she had left was moving up and, with a smile at a motherly woman who had been standing behind her, she slipped back into her place, saying, 'Pray, wait for me by that bench. I do not think I shall be long.'

As she waited to be handed her package, she pondered this new information. Guisborough's wife was ill, Guisborough's heir was ill. It really seemed as though there were a curse on the family, as the country people said. Then she scolded herself for being nonsensical. Whatever ailed little Michael Sullivan could have no connection with the malady that had seized both Lady Guisboroughs. Could it?

At that moment, the harried clerk handed her a small box, which she slipped into her reticule. Dominic may have forgotten the anniversary of their marriage, but she had not. She rather looked forward to the moment when he would realize his omission and how she would make him suffer for it, until that is, she allowed him to make it up to her in his own inimitable way.

Smiling to herself, she crossed the room to where the Sullivan family awaited her. She perceived Thomas standing by the bench, his arms crossed over his chest. 'Thomas, is the carriage outside?'

'At the door, my lady.'

'Very good.' She turned to Mrs Sullivan. 'Please step this way.'

Maria Sullivan stood, but held her hand to her forehead as though she were giddy. Her husband let go of his son's hand and caught her as she half fainted. There was a little hubbub, people pressed close. Then, Cecily heard the little boy wail, 'Mama!' and saw him being born off by a shabby person whose face, even on this hot day, was hidden by a muffler.

'Thomas! Stop them!' she called, pointing at the retreating figures. The groom sprang into action and, in a few moments, had thrust his way through the throng and out into the street. Thomas stood head-and-shoulders above the rest of the crowd and soon sighted the man striding down the street with the weeping child in his arms. He sprinted after then and, coming up with the man, wrested the child from his grip. With his arms full of the distraught little boy, he was unable to keep his hold on the assailant and, by the time the boy's father came up to them, the ragged man had disappeared into the crowds on the high street.

Cecily came running up. 'Well done, oh, well done!' she said, almost embracing the groom in her enthusiasm. 'You were splendid.' Then, turning to the father, she said, 'Is the child hurt?'

'No, Ma'am, thanks to you and your servant. Will you take hold of him while I go back to my wife? She will be in such anxiety.'

'Of course. We will wait for you in the carriage.' She lifted the child into the chaise and sank back against the blue, leather squabs. Goodness, that had been a close thing! She noticed that the little boy was very pale and strangely silent. This was, obviously, an occasion for sugarplums. She had purchased a box for Bobby, but what he had never had, he would not miss. She selected a gaily packaged box from the formidable pile of packages on the opposite seat and untied the ribbon around the box, which she proffered to Michael. A little sunshine beamed in the child's eyes as he made his careful choice. The pinched, scared look disappeared, and the threatened storm of tears was averted.

Absently stroking the little boy's hair, Cecily stared out of the carriage window with unseeing eyes. She turned over the events of the past few days in her mind, and slowly, dimly, a pattern began to emerge.

Thirteen: Where the Bee Sucks

'You say his face was muffled?' said Dominic, thoughtfully. 'So it could have been anyone.'

'Yes,' acknowledged Cecily. 'He had a muffler over his mouth and a hat pulled over his eyes and even gloves.'

'Ah! That is very interesting.'

'Why?'

'Think about it. Why did he need to hide his hands? Could it be that they would have betrayed him? It is hard to disguise a gentleman's hands. You can dirty them, certainly, but ragged nails, and calluses cannot be conjured all in a moment. And, if they could, he would not be able to rid himself of them and appear in his own character the very same day.'

'Very true. But we've always known it was a gentleman, haven't we?'

'Or a nobleman,' he reminded her.

'No—I do not think that any longer. Lord Guisborough could have no reason to kidnap his own heir. It is nonsense.'

'I would rather like to talk to these Sullivans.' His voice was thoughtful. 'Where did you take them?'

'They have lodgings in Queen Street. Not a very nice street, and not very nice rooms. I think they are quite badly off, poor things.'

'And so they have come to see what Cousin Guisborough will do for them.'

'You need not sound so superior.' Cecily was inclined to be indignant.

'I don't like spongers.'

'But they are not like that at all!'

'Let me judge for myself,' he told her as he placed her shawl around her shoulders. 'It isn't far. We'll walk.'

The Sullivan family had taken lodgings above a chandler's shop in Queen Street. It was not at all dissimilar to those that Cecily and her mama had occupied in London before her engagement as nursery governess to young Lord Fanshawe. There was, she reflected, wrinkling her nose, the same smell of boiled cabbage and mouse droppings that seemed inseparable from furnished lodgings everywhere. They climbed four sets of stairs to reach the top floor of the house and found themselves outside a freshly painted door with a well-polished brass knocker. A card tacked to the wall beside the knocker was simply inscribed 'Sullivan.'

Dominic rapped briskly upon the door. There was silence for a few moments. Then, just as he lifted the knocker again, the door was opened by a diminutive maidservant, a little out of breath.

'Yessir?'

'Good afternoon. Is your mistress at home?'

'Yes—no—I dunno,' was the answer. 'Mistress is with Master Michael—he's poorly.'

'Major Sullivan then? Pray, take him my card.'

'Aye, the Master's in,' she said, wiping her hands on her apron before taking the card. 'Step in a minute, and I'll see.'

She opened the door to allow them into a narrow entrance hall and scuttled off, mouse-like, into the back rooms. There came a murmur of voices, and then a man's figure emerged into the light.

'Good God! It's Mick Sullivan!' Dominic strode forward to grip the other man's hand and slap his shoulder several times. 'Mick Sullivan! You old dog. Where've you sprung from?'

Sullivan was smiling. 'Dom! How are you?'

'The better for seeing you! Cecily, allow me introduce Major Michael Sullivan, late of the Irish Rifles and the best comrade a man could have.'

It was obvious to Cecily that there would be no more talk of 'spongers' from her husband. Also that, unless she reminded him, her husband and the Major would be happy to reminisce over old times without coming to the point at all.

'Major Sullivan—' she managed to interpose during a brief lull in the conversation—'I do not wish to appear impertinent; pray believe I have a reason for asking. How long have you been in Lincolnshire? And why have you come?'

He turned to her, the laughter wiped from his lips. 'We are here because of our boy, Ma'am. Our little Michael. He has been ailing for some time now, and our doctor in Kildare has not the skill, cannot even find the cause. I came over myself to sound out Guisborough—Damn it! He must have some concern for his heir's health—But he put me off with promises. I gather he has problems of his own at the moment.'

'What is it you want him to do?' asked Cecily.

'We consulted a doctor in London. He says that Michael would benefit from a warmer climate and cleaner air. We want to take him to Switzerland—but—I do not know how we are to live there. It is hard enough to make ends meet in Ireland.' He grinned at Dominic. 'The proverbial Irish bogtrotters, that's us. My dear wife joined me with Michael last month, and we have been waiting for word from Guisborough ever since. I am hoping that Doctor Stewart will stand our friend.'

'Doctor Stewart? You know him?'

'We have not met, but we have corresponded. Guisborough consulted him when he first got my letter. Stewart has been most kind, even discovering the name of a physician in Geneva under whom we could place the boy.'

'Has he examined Michael?'

'No, but he sent some good advice.'

Cecily gave a most unladylike snort. 'I wager I know what his advice was—"Cream, eggs, honey, liver, and sweetbreads. That is the best medicine."'

The Major laughed. 'I see you know the good doctor. I suppose it cannot hurt.'

'It will not be much help if what he really needs is to go abroad. And the air here, with all the smoke and dust of the town, cannot be good for him.'

From the open door of a back room, presumably a bedchamber, a pretty, untrained voice was singing in the soft, rhythmic cadence of a lullaby:

'Honey though the bee prepares,
An envenomed sting he wears;
Piercing thorns a guard compose
Round the fragrant blooming rose.

Where we think to find a sweet,
Oft a painful sting we meet:
When the rose invites our eye,
We forget the thorn is nigh.'

'Your wife has a lovely voice,' commented Dominic. 'I hope to meet her soon, but now I think we should leave you. This is obviously not a good time for a social call.'

The Major stood and held out his hand once more. 'It has done me a power of good to see you again, old fellow. One gets rather too caught up in things. Begin to imagine—but never mind that.'

'Imagine what?' said Dominic, his eyes searching the other man's face. 'Tell me, Mick.'

Sullivan made a grimace and laughed a little. 'Well, that—that—someone—is trying to do us harm.'

'The man who tried to abduct your son, for example.'

'That—and other things. An accident to our carriage on the journey from Liverpool—my wife almost trampled by a runaway horse in the street—and I was set upon by footpads just outside these lodgings.'

Dominic looked thoughtful. But all he said was, 'Lincoln can be a rough place. Why don't you come to stay with us in Alford? Then perhaps these—accidents—will not occur.'

'Do you mean it?' cried Sullivan with a sudden flush of pleasure. 'Dom, you don't know how much that would mean to me and to Maria.'

'Then we'll consider it settled. How long will it take you to pack?'

Sullivan glanced around vaguely. 'I don't know. Not long. Pretty much everything in here belongs to the landlord.'

'Then Cecily and I will return to the Red Lion and wait for you. We can take you back with us in the chaise.'

In accordance with these plans, Dominic and Cecily returned to the inn and, as Dominic realised that the afternoon was well advanced and he had not eaten since an early breakfast, he ordered a substantial repast. The hostelry prided itself on catering for the gentry, and the meal presently set before them comprised a fricassee of veal, a raised pigeon pie, baked carp in aspic, stuffed and roasted quail, and oyster stew. Dominic was not, however, permitted to enjoy his dinner in peace.

'You never told me you were acquainted with the Sullivans,' said Cecily, eyeing him rather severely.

'I didn't know that I was,' he protested. 'There must be hundreds of Michael Sullivans in Ireland. I didn't even know he had sold out. If I thought about it at all, I assumed he was still with the army of occupation.'

'You knew he was married?'

'Yes, but you don't suppose he gave me his wife's genealogy, do you?'

She accepted this and turned her attention to a morsel of veal. 'This is very good.' After a short silence, she said, 'It is too much of a coincidence.'

'What is?'

'Little Michael's illness. I believe it is all part of the plot.'

He took a sip of his wine. 'I've been wondering about that myself. But I don't see how. Unless one accepts that there is yet another heir waiting in the wings who is committed to the wholesale murder of anyone who stands between him and the title, born or unborn.'

'Well, why not?'

'Because it's ludicrous. And remember, my dear girl, we have already established that the murderer must be someone so familiar with the Park that his comings and goings arouse no suspicion at all. Someone completely accepted by the family and the household.'

'Well?'

'Don't you think Guisborough would be aware of it if Stewart or Tweedie or—Lord help us—the apothecary, was so close a connection?'

She sighed. 'I suppose so. But still, it is queer. What about all the accidents and that terrible man who tried to steal the boy.'

'Yes, that is suspicious. But such things do happen.'

'You don't really believe that,' she said shrewdly. 'Or else, why did you invite them to your grandmother's house?'

'I think,' he said firmly, 'that it is better to be safe than sorry.'

Fourteen: An Unexpected Visitor

Cecily was secretly very much relieved when the chaise eventually clattered into the graveled driveway in front of Maythorpe Manor. The journey, with an exhausted mother, over-excited little boy, and preoccupied father, had not been an enlivening one. Dominic, too, was unusually quiet, or perhaps, she thought rather waspishly, he was simply sleeping off the effects of his gargantuan dinner. It was now past eight o'clock, and the daylight was disappearing rapidly, not only due to the setting sun but also to ominous, dark clouds that hid the moon. As they stepped down, the long threatened rain began to fall.

'Oh, thank goodness!' she cried when she saw the front door open and the butler step forth holding an umbrella. 'Dear Mrs Sullivan, we are home, and you have nothing more to concern you. Should you like to eat supper with Michael in his room or downstairs with us?'

Maria Sullivan smiled and said with an effort, 'You are very kind. I think we would both be better for our beds. My husband—'

'Have no fear. He shall have supper as soon as may be.'

'Thank you. If you only knew the comfort—!'

To Cecily's dismay, she saw tears start in the other woman's eyes, and she caught her two hands between her own. 'Do not—pray do not! We are so happy to have you with us! Why, your husband and mine are such old friends, we must be friends, too. And when Michael is better, we shall drive into Alford, and he shall meet my nephew Bobby and all the vicarage children.'

Talking cheerfully all the way, she escorted Maria and the child upstairs to the bedchambers that had been hurriedly prepared for them. Thomas had been sent ahead of the party with a message to the housekeeper, and this formidable dame had risen to the occasion admirably. There were fires in the rooms, fresh linen scented with lavender on the beds, and pitchers of hot water on the wash stands.

Cecily glanced around with approval. 'I will have supper brought up to you,' she said. 'Is there anything in particular you would like me to order for Michael?'

'Oh, just some bread and butter and perhaps a boiled egg,' said Maria gratefully. 'Oh, and a glass of hot milk if you please.'

'And for you?'

'Nothing, I thank you. I shall do very well.'

'Nonsense. I know there was a fricassee of chicken for dinner, and a ragout of veal. And I think you should have a glass of wine too.'

As they waited for the food to arrive, Mrs Sullivan laid out Michael's medicine bottles, his tonic, a jar of honey, his toothbrush, and other necessities of life that soothed the child with their familiarity.

When the footman appeared with a laden tray, Maria took the glass of milk and carefully stirred in a spoonful of honey. 'Michael will not drink it without something to sweeten it.'

'And why should he?' said Cecily with a smile. 'My nephew always complains about the horrid skin that forms on the top. Well, I will leave you in peace now, but do please ring if there is anything else you need.'

By the time she returned to the drawing room, Major Sullivan had already retired, leaving Dominic and Cecily to a blissful half-hour in front of the fire. Cecily sat, contentedly, with her head on her husband's shoulder while he smoothed the disordered curls and occasionally turned up her face for a kiss. They talked, as they had not talked in many days, about private, intimate matters—little confidences and words of love to bind their marriage closer.

Dominic had just intimated that it was time for bed, with a look that even now could bring a blush to his wife's face, when there came a wild rapping at the front door.

'Good gracious, are we never to have an evening in peace?' Cecily said in a disgusted tone. Then she looked at her husband with quick alarm. 'Do you think—Isabella—?'

But it was not a messenger from the Park who called so late and in such weather. They reached the front door just as Fothergill cautiously opened it, peering out into the night. 'Who's there?'

They could hardly hear the answer. But, with a horrified exclamation, the butler appeared to catch the late visitor in his arms and half staggered into the entrance hall. Clinging to his chest, dripping and shivering like a drowned cat, was Alana Stewart.

Cecily ran forward to take the girl from the affronted butler's arms. 'Alana—Alana, my dear—what does this mean?'

The girl lifted her head and parted the dripping hair that matted her forehead. 'I did not know where else to go—you were so kind—I am so afraid!'

Dominic, who had been standing frozen with surprise, strode forward. 'Come into the drawing room, Miss—Stewart is it? You are chilled to the bone. Fothergill, is there any of the soup we had for supper in the kitchen still? Good—fetch a bowl for the lady, will you?'

He followed his wife and her strange visitor into the room. Cecily had already stripped the dripping cloak from Alana's tiny frame and wrapped a shawl of her own around her. 'There, my dear,' she said, gently pushing the girl into a chair near the fire. She dropped to her knees beside her and took the cold hands in hers to chafe some warmth into them. 'Now— tell me why you have come to us.'

This command was not easily obeyed. Alana seemed quite unable to order her thoughts or command her tongue. For several minutes, she simply sat, rocking herself to and fro, while her teeth chattered and the tears fell copiously. Dominic muttered something about 'seeing about that soup' and very meanly left his wife to cope with the situation.

Cecily murmured soothingly to the girl as she smoothed the wet hair and patted her hands. Eventually, when this proved inefficacious, she directed her in stern accents to pull herself together. Rather to her surprise, this worked. Alana sat a little straighter, ceased her rocking, and wiped her eyes.

'Oh, I do beg your pardon. What must you think of me?'

'Only that something very terrible has happened to distress you. Tell me all about it.'

Just then, Dominic entered the room, followed by Fothergill with a bowl of soup and some sandwiches upon a salver. These he set down on a small table that he drew up beside Alana's chair. With a gentleness that his wife thought very charming, Dominic spread a white napkin over the girl's lap and handed her a spoon. 'This will make you feel better.'

'Oh, thank you,' she whispered with a gasp. She sipped some of the steaming bouillon and nibbled the corner of a sandwich. 'You are both so kind.'

Cecily was, by this time, almost dancing with impatience. But she kept her voice low and calm, just as she might have spoken to Bobby if he had come to her in tears. 'Now, do you think you can tell us what has happened?'

Alana sniffed and nodded. She set down her spoon and took a deep breath. 'Well, I had just stepped out of the house—it was a lovely evening until the rain, you know—and Mr Repton—happened—to be passing by and—'

Cecily smiled. 'You do not have to prevaricate with us, you know. You slipped out to meet him, didn't you?'

Alana dropped her eyes and nodded.

'Well, that is very romantic, to be sure.'

A little smile curved the childlike mouth. 'Yes—it was.' She looked up suddenly, her eyes kindling. 'But there was nothing wrong in it! Whatever Hector says!'

'Doctor Stewart saw you?'

'No, it was one of the servants. My brother sets them on to spy on me in the most humiliating way and, when he came home, he was in such anger—' She stopped, her voice suspended by tears.

'You cannot blame him for that,' interposed Dominic. 'Repton should have known better—your reputation—'

Cecily, remembering a certain scene in a moonlit garden in the course of their own romance, turned away, biting her lip to hide a smile.

'He—he accused me of—of allowing—allowing—but I never did and John would not. He is the soul of honour and he—loves me.'

Dominic, never one to mince words said, 'He accused Repton of seducing you?'

'Yes—and he said I would be ruined and no one would ever want to—to—marry me. And I said that John would, and Hector said men never marry girls who let them—you know. And—oh, Sir Dominic—he has gone after John with a horsewhip, and he says he will take care he does not boast of his conquest around the county—!' She jumped suddenly from her chair and ran to Dominic, flinging herself at his feet. 'Sir Dominic, don't let him hurt John—I beg you—go after him.'

'But, my dear, I have no right to interfere. And surely, Mr Repton is young and strong. Is it not more likely that he will end by turning the whip upon your brother?'

'No! You do not know Hector. He can be terrible! Terrible!'

Cecily bent over and patted Alana on the shoulder. 'Calm yourself, my dear. You will make yourself ill. Of course Dominic will go.'

Dominic cast his wife a reproachful look, then disengaged the little hands that clung to his. 'Very well. I will do what I can, but I have no doubt they will both send me to the devil.'

He rang for Fothergill and requested that his horse be saddled and brought around to the front of the house. There was silence in the room for a few minutes while Alana sipped her soup. Cecily could think of nothing to say, while Dominic was aggrieved and inclined to blame Cecily for being altogether too kind-hearted.

When Fothergill returned to inform him gravely that his horse was saddled and at the door, he got up and cast a disgruntled look out of the window at the still-lashing rain. 'Come, help me into my coat, Cecily.'

This was a sufficiently unusual command to ensure Cecily's obedience. So, rather than telling him to get himself into his own coat, she got up and, with a reassuring word to Alana, followed him from the room.

'This is a damned odd business,' he said without preamble. 'What do you make of it?'

'I told you she was afraid of him,' Cecily reminded her husband.

'And I told you that doesn't make him a murderer.' He frowned. 'Did he strike you as the kind of stern, Calvinistic Scott who would be enraged by a harmless little romance?'

'No, but men are often very protective of their sisters and daughters, I believe.'

'Yes, but—but—the girl is hardly seen in the village, never visits and, as far as I know, never attends the assemblies in Lincoln. How does he intend to marry her off if she is kept so close? And besides, you would have thought young Repton would be a very good match for a country doctor's sister.'

'Are you acquainted with him?'

'No, not to speak to, but I know of the family, and I have met the old man. He is a manufacturer, but perfectly well-bred.'

'I thought the young man very gentlemanlike, too. And I should certainly dislike to see his handsome face spoiled by a whip—so off you go, my hero, and rescue him.' She patted him kindly on the back and gave him a little shove.

'Oh, very well.' He nodded to Fothergill, who opened the front door, letting in a sudden gust of icy wind and rainwater. 'I shall catch my death!' he protested. Then he hunched his shoulders, pulled his hat over his eyes, and walked resolutely out into the storm.

Cecily stood watching him as he was swallowed up into the darkness. She had no real fears for him. Her Dominic was more than capable of dealing with whatever awaited him. She turned with a sigh back to the little parlour where Alana was waiting for her.

'He has gone,' she said with a smile. 'There is nothing for you to worry about now.'

'It is my fault—all my fault!' cried the girl, her voice rising with incipient hysteria. 'If John is hurt before Sir Dominic can—'

'Nonsense,' said Cecily in a voice calculated to check the rising tide. 'You make too much of it. No one will get hurt. And, as for it being your fault—that is nonsense, too. If your brother had not kept you mewed up in that house, never meeting anyone—why, you were practically bound to fall in love with the first young man you met. Now, when my friend Isabella is well again, there will be parties at the Park, and you may meet him there in a perfectly respectable way, and—'

'She will never be well. Hector says so. And he says she is a foolish, nervous creature—not worthy of the Earl.'

'Does he, indeed?' Cecily was indignant. 'Well, I have known her since we were children, and I can tell you he is quite wrong. I have met the Earl, and I do not think he is so very—'

'He is the handsomest, most charming, kindest, and best man I have ever known,' interrupted Alana.

Cecily was silenced. She was sure she had heard those very words before. Yes—only yesterday. And uttered in that strange sing-song voice, too.

'But surely,' she said in a reasonable voice, 'it is Mr Repton who is all those things. You are in love with him, not the Earl.'

Alana's eyes widened. She looked bewildered. 'What did you say?'

'I said, it is Mr Repton that you love—is it not?'

'Yes, oh yes!'

'And the Earl is—'

'He is the handsomest, most charm—'

Cecily could never afterwards explain the impulse that

caused her to spring forward and slap the girl sharply on either cheek with the palm of her hand. There was something so horrible and unnatural in that repetition that she felt that she must stop it at all costs. 'Do not say that!' she said, with authority. 'It is not true, and you know it!'

Alana stared at her and, even as Cecily watched, a different look came into her eyes. They lost their glazed, unfocussed stare and fixed themselves on Cecily's face. 'Why do you say that? What is not true? What did I say?'

'What you always say whenever the Earl is mentioned: that he is handsome, and charming, and all that is wonderful. All I can say is that he may be a very good sort of man, but he is no paragon.'

'Oh, I know. He is quite old and dreadfully dull. He never talks of anything interesting or says pretty things. I feel quite sorry for his poor little wife.'

Cecily stared at her. There was something most strange and sinister going on here. It became apparent to her that Isabella was not the only young woman who was being controlled—by means unspecified—for some dreadful purpose.

Fifteen: The Brother, the Lover, and the Knight

As Dominic set his indignant mount through the driving rain
and fierce winds, he reflected upon his dearly loved—and
exasperating—spouse. He was well aware that, in spite of her
teasing and mockery, she regarded him as a hero, and he
endeavoured to live up to her image of him. But he had never
felt less like a hero and would have given much to be snug and
warm in his own bed—with his adoring wife beside him.
Moreover, he felt that he would make a very bad third in the
quarrel between the outraged doctor and the young lover, who
was undoubtedly behaving in a dashed havey-cavey way.
Whether Alana was justified in keeping their attachment from
her brother, Dominic could not pretend to judge. But he felt
that young Repton would have done better to call openly at
the cottage and pay his addresses in the usual way.

At this point in his musings, the clouds parted, and the
moon appeared, shedding silver light upon a rain-washed
landscape. To his left, Dominic could just see the towers of
Coningsby Park, stark and menacing against the leaden sky.
Surely, the doctor's house must be quite near? Yes, there was
a faint light from an unshuttered window. Dominic slipped
from the saddle and tied the reins to a convenient fence post.
Then he stalked towards the house, wondering how he was to
account for his presence.

The rain had not quite ceased, but it was no longer
whipping against his face or blinding his eyes. It was quiet
now, after the storm. There came the faint sound of man's
voice insistently calling Repton by name. Dominic made his
way towards the sound. Presently, he broke through a thicket
and came upon a clearing in the wood. Doctor Stewart was
bending over a figure slumped upon the crushed ferns, in the
act of feeling for a pulse.

'Good God, what is this?' demanded Dominic striding
forward. 'What have you done?'

The doctor spun around. 'Cavendish? Thank God you
have come, man. Help me get him inside.'

Dominic stared at him. 'But—what have you done to him?'

The doctor returned his puzzled stare. 'I? Nothing. I found him as you see him, a few moments before you arrived.'

'Unconscious?'

'Aye. I have done my best to rouse him. But to no avail. He's taken a sad blow to the head, poor fellow.'

Dominic raised an eyebrow and directed a significant look at the heavy silver head of the doctor's cane. 'Indeed?'

'My dear Sir, you do not imagine that I—? Never mind that now. We must get him inside. He is soaked to the skin, and in his weakened condition, I fear—'

'I have seen men in a worse case,' remarked Dominic, picking up the young gentleman's feet with a shrug. 'He seems a healthy specimen. He'll survive.'

Stewart lifted Repton's shoulders without effort. 'No doubt. But he is subject to severe chest colds—has been since a boy.'

It had not previously occurred to Dominic that Stewart might be the Repton family's physician. It made the Doctor's attitude the more incomprehensible. He must know that the young man was not only thoroughly respectable, but heir to a not inconsiderable fortune.

They carried their burden across the Doctor's neat lawn and in through the long, open windows of the little parlour. 'There, lay him upon the sofa. Stay—let me pull off his boots.'

Dominic watched this operation with a grin. 'Your housekeeper will have something to say about this.' He waved his hand towards the trails of muddy footprints on the polished floor.'

Stewart laughed. 'Indeed, she will. Though it is easier to clean up than blood.'

'You get much of that?'

'My dear Sir, every injured labourer in the district, makes for this house.'

'It must be disagreeable for your sister.'

'I keep her away from that side of things as much as possible. She is, as you will have guessed, delicate and easily overset.' He glanced at the youth on the sofa, who was turning his head slightly upon the cushion. He seemed almost to awake, than sank back into unconsciousness 'I am glad she had retired for the night before this happened.'

Dominic hesitated but reflected that he could not keep Alana's whereabouts a secret from her brother. 'In point of fact, Stewart, she did not. You must know she is at the Manor with my wife. She ran through the storm to tell us of your—disagreement—and begged me to intercede between you and Repton. It was not a commission I relished, but—'

'Oh, for God's sake!' The doctor looked thoroughly put out. 'Is there to be no end to this! What pray did she tell you I was going to do?'

'Er—take a horsewhip to him, I believe.'

'What? A boy I've known since he was breeched? He sighed and suddenly sank into a chair, motioning Dominic to take a seat opposite. 'Listen, Cavendish—can you hold your tongue?'

'Certainly.' He might have added that holding his tongue was an integral part of his job, but he held his peace.

The doctor took a deep breath and began to speak as though the words were forced out of him. 'Everyone—Lady Cavendish—Guisborough—the villagers—they all believe that I brought Alana here to keep house for me.' He looked up sharply. 'Surely, you, at least, can see that she is quite incapable of managing a household—?'

Dominic smiled and said in a placatory tone, 'She is very young, after all.'

'She is five-and-twenty.'

'As much as that? I had not thought it. But I met her only briefly; she was much distressed—'

The doctor interrupted him. 'I brought Alana here to keep her—and others—safe!'

'Safe?'

'Did your wife tell you how Alana and Repton met?'

'Why, yes—some romantic tale of a rabbit in a trap. Young Repton rode to the rescue like any knight errant and reaped the usual reward.'

'Cavendish—understand this. It was well for that rabbit that Repton came upon the scene. Its death at Alana's hands would not have been—pretty.'

Dominic's brows drew together in a quick frown. 'What is that you say?' he said in a voice filled with distaste.

'It began years ago. My mother's cat, my father's favourite hack, a tame robin that would eat from her hand. It took us a long time to discover the truth. My sister has the face of an angel—and most of the time, that is exactly what she is—a sweet, innocent child. Then these urges will come upon her, and—'

'Good God! No wonder you keep her close.'

'It is this house, or a lunatic asylum.' The doctor's voice was unutterably weary. 'It may come to that. Lately, she has been getting out more frequently. She is very cunning, you see, and I do not know where she goes. She seems to be—satisfied—in some way when she returns. That worries me more than I can tell you.'

A movement and a muffled groan from the sofa reminded the two men that they were not alone. Stewart stood quickly and strode across the room to where the youth was stirring. He looked keenly down into the handsome young face, seemed satisfied, and turned aside to pour some brandy into a glass. 'Here, drink this, my lad.'

Repton struggled onto one elbow and took the glass in his free hand. He sipped cautiously and coughed as the fiery spirit caught him in the throat. 'God! My head—what happened?'

'We were about to ask you the same question,' interposed Dominic, coming to stand by Stewart's shoulder. 'You were struck down—by whom we do not know. Do you?'

Repton set down the glass and pressed his hand to his face. 'Who are—? Oh, it's Cavendish, isn't it? How comes it that you are here?'

'I cannot see that it matters. But, if it troubles you, I came at Miss Stewart's behest. She—er—feared for your safety.'

'But—why?'

'Because, you young fool, I discovered that you and she had been meeting, clandestinely, in my woods,' said Stewart in a grim voice.

Young Mr Repton flushed and sank back against the sofa cushions. 'I know, Sir; it was very bad. I would have come to speak to you weeks ago, but—Alana—would not let me. I think she likes the romance—the secrecy. She is such a child.'

Dominic was amused to hear his own sentiments thus repeated, but Stewart did not correct them in this instance. He merely said, 'You, on the other hand, are not a child, and you must know how dishonourable your conduct has been.'

'I do. But I never—I mean, my intentions—I want to marry your sister, Sir.'

'You have still to tell us why Doctor Stewart found you unconscious in the wood. What were you doing there? According to Miss Stewart, you had parted some time before.'

'I received a note begging me to return. She seemed to be in such distress. I hastened to the little spinney where we were used to meet. You know what the weather was like—I was dashed nervous, to be honest, for the storm was directly overhead then and the lightning forking right above me.'

'Very intrepid of you to remain,' remarked Dominic, faintly sardonic.

'Well, Sir, everyone knows you should not stand under a tree in a thunderstorm.'

'As I said, very intrepid. What happened next?'

'Well, I could not hear anything for the thunder and the rain. But someone called my name, very low, and I spun around and just caught a glimpse of a figure in a cloak with a hood pulled down and then—nothing!'

'Was it a man or a woman?'

'I don't know. I tell you, I was half blinded by the storm.

But, surely, no woman would do such a thing?'

'I have known women who would strike a man down without a second thought,' said Dominic with a laugh. 'But it doesn't seem likely in this case.' He looked thoughtfully at Doctor Stewart. 'How long would you say he had been unconscious when you found him, Stewart?'

'Impossible to say in this weather. He was cold and clammy to the touch, but that would be the rain. Perhaps half-an-hour. Possibly less, but not, I think, any longer.'

Dominic looked very thoughtful. 'I wonder—I wonder—'

'What?'

'Oh—my apologies—it occurred to me that perhaps this was an attempt to injure *you* Doctor Stewart. Rather than young Repton.'

'I do not understand you, Sir.'

'Only that, if the blow had proved fatal, you might have found it extremely tricky to prove your innocence.'

'Good God,' said the doctor, blankly. 'But why?'

'You are Lady Guisborough's medical man,' Dominic reminded him. 'I can imagine you are a thorn in the side of whoever wishes to do her harm.'

'But that is insane!'

'Oh, yes, I think we can take it that whoever is behind these occurrences is quite out of his mind.'

Sixteen: Lady Cavendish Receives a Summons

After all the excitements of the previous day, Cecily felt quite unable to face her various guests over the breakfast table. She, therefore, followed the Dowager's example and breakfasted off a tray in her bedchamber. Dominic, visiting her as she leaned back against her pillows, reported that the other ladies had elected to do the same, and so only he and Major Sullivan had partaken of a hearty meal of beef and ham washed down with tankards of porter. Cecily shuddered and sipped her coffee.

Dominic smiled at her and murmured that she looked very fetching in her pretty lace dressing gown, but his manner was a trifle distracted. He gestured with a letter that lay open in his hand. 'I have to go back to London for a couple of days, sweetheart. The Minister wants to meet Raoul in person before he lets him loose with a frigate, a full crew, and a brigade of marines. I can't say that I blame him.'

Cecily's face fell. 'Oh, bother the Minister! Just when we are in the middle of an investigation!'

He laughed. 'And I thought you were pulling that long face because you will miss me.'

'Pooh! I am not so poor a creature that I cannot live without my husband for two days—or even longer.' She relented and reached out a hand to him across the cracked eggshells on her plate. 'But not very much longer, darling Dominic.'

He clasped her hand. 'I'd better tell you now, I suppose—I shall have to go out to West Africa with him on his first voyage. Just as an observer, you know.'

'Shall we?'

He lifted her hand to his lips and kissed it. 'Yes, *we* shall.' A sudden thought occurred. 'Now listen to me—you are not to do any more investigating while I'm away.'

'Why? What harm can it do just to talk to people?'

'It could do a great deal of harm if one of the people you choose to talk to is a cold-blooded killer. If he or she—'

'Please don't start that again!'

'All right. If the *murderer* suspects you are on to him, he might not wait to make sure before taking action.'

Cecily put her head on one side, considering. 'Well, I promise not to investigate anyone until you come back. But I do want to visit Isabella. After all, that cannot be dangerous, everyone knows I'm an old friend.'

He looked at her suspiciously. 'Have you got some plan you haven't told me about?'

She raised innocent eyes to his face. 'Dominic! I can't believe you would ask me such a thing.'

'Now I know you do.'

'It is just that, I thought perhaps I could take Alana with me to visit at the Park. It would be very interesting to see how she reacts to Lord Guisborough. I cannot help wondering if the spell is truly broken—'

He shook his head. 'No, Cecily. Alana must return to her brother at once.' His voice was unusually stern.

'But why?'

Dominic had given a promise of secrecy to Stewart, but he had no intention of keeping the truth from his wife. He related just what Stewart had told him. 'I believe it was she that struck John Repton down before she turned up at our door.'

Cecily was very much shocked. 'I cannot believe it!'

'Nevertheless, I am not going to leave you here with her. Promise me she goes home this morning.'

'I promise,' she said, slipping out of bed to stand on tiptoe to kiss his chin. 'Do you have to leave right away?'

'No, Raoul is not here yet. He is driving us up to Town in his curricle,' he answered absently. Then, noting her smile, his face lightened, and he said, running his hands up the length of her bare arms, 'Which gives us time to say goodbye properly.'

'Or improperly,' murmured Cecily as she surrendered her lips to his.

* * * *

An hour later, Cecily waved her handkerchief after Saint Michel's curricle until it was out of sight, wiped a tear from her eye, and went off to belatedly visit her guests. Major Sullivan had ridden into Lincoln on business; and, as the Dowager never left her chamber until noon, only Alana, Mrs Stewart, and little Michael occupied the morning room.

They made a pretty group: Alana, divinely blond; Maria Sullivan, a dark Irish beauty; and the delicate little boy, with flaxen curls and too large, brown eyes. Three faces were turned to her with varying degrees of alarm as she walked into the room. How nervous they all were, she thought, puzzled. She was wondering how to follow her husband's last adjuration to send Alana home—really one could not just turf a guest out of the house—when Alana solved the problem for her.

'Dear Lady Cavendish, I have been waiting—I must go home, and I wanted to thank you before I go. You have been so very, very kind. And Sir Dominic, too, for bringing me such comfortable news of Mr Repton.'

'Oh, that was nothing. But how shall you go? Has your brother sent a carriage for you?'

'No—no—I shall walk. It is not far, you know, if one takes the paths across the fields.'

'But, after all that rain! The way will be so muddy! Let me send you home in our chaise.'

'Really, I would so much rather walk,' said the girl, her lips beginning to tremble.

'Of course, if that is what you want,' said Cecily, reflecting that the girl was so hedged about with restrictions that it must be a relief for her to do as she wished occasionally. Then she remembered what Dominic had told her about the rabbit and shivered a little. She could not believe it—but, if it should be true, the sooner Alana was at a distance from Michael, the better.

She breathed more easily when she had seen Alana off the

premises. With apologies to Mrs Sullivan, she went about some of the household duties that the Dowager had been only too glad to relinquish to her; and no sooner had she finished these tasks, than a message arrived, by the carrier, from Kate Leonard with good news: Lion was recovering well, the tube had been removed from his throat, and he was breathing normally again.

She sat down to write a note of congratulation to Kate. She had written no more than the salutation when she was disturbed by the sound of a horse galloping along the driveway. This was so unusual that she jumped up from her writing desk, convinced that some accident had befallen her beloved Dominic.

When she reached the entrance hall, Fothergill was already at the door. 'A message from Coningsby Park, my Lady, for the young master.'

Cecily peered around his portly figure to see a groom, in Coningsby livery, standing on the shallow, stone steps. 'If you please, Ma'am,' said this youth, spying Cecily in the shadow, 'Miss Proudie says if his Lordship is out of the house, could you come yourself. I was to tell you it is desperate urgent, she says.'

'Oh, good Lord, what has happened?'

'Mistress has gone missin', Ma'am. An' the house all in an uproar. That's all I know.'

'Pray, ride back to the Park as quick as you can and tell Miss Proudie I will be there directly. Fothergill, send one of the grooms after Sir Dominic and ask him to meet me at the Park. Tell him it is a matter of life and death! I will take the barouche.'

'Driving yourself, my lady?'

'No, one of the grooms must drive me.' Dominic had attempted to impart his skill with the ribbons to his bride; but, as every lesson had ended in a violent quarrel and tears, they had decided that it was really quite unnecessary for her to learn to drive. As Cecily climbed into the barouche, she glared

135

resentfully at the groom's back and registered a vow to resume her lessons—but not with Dominic—as soon as they returned to London.

It had been a fine morning; but, as so often happens, by the time the barouche swung into the circular drive in front of Coningsby Park, the clouds were once more lowering over the house. Cecily shivered and wished she had worn a pelisse. She pulled her shawl around her shoulders and, holding the thin, black silk with one hand, she accepted a footman's assistance and descended the step onto the gravel.

Hardly had she entered the great hall, when Miss Proudie appeared. Cecily's eyes opened wide at the sight of her. Her former schoolmistress' face was grey, and she looked twenty years older than when Cecily had last seen her. Matters must be desperate, indeed!

'Dear Ma'am, you are not well!' cried Cecily, running forward to grasp the elderly lady's hands. She felt them tremble and realised that Miss Proudie was on the brink of collapse. 'Sit down,' she said, pressing the lady into a nearby chair. She turned to the butler, who was hovering in an agitated manner, 'Pray, bring some brandy at once.'

He bowed, glad to have something to do, and within a very short space of time returned with a decanter in one hand and a glass in the other. Cecily perceived that he, too, was shaking and had not trusted himself to carry a tray.

She held the brandy glass to Miss Proudie's lips and was pleased to see a little colour return to her cheeks as she swallowed. 'Now, please tell me what has happened.'

Miss Proudie struggled to compose herself and presently began in a determinedly unemotional tone. 'This morning, when the maidservant took Lady Guisborough's breakfast tray to her room, she found the bed unoccupied and Nurse asleep in her chair. She could not wake her—drugged of course—and though we have searched and searched the house and the grounds—Isabella is still missing.'

Cecily sat for a moment, digesting this news, then

absently finished the brandy in Miss Proudie's glass. 'Who saw Isabella last, and at what time? Apart from Nurse, I mean.'

'One of the lower servants, a nice girl, went in at six o'clock to clear the grate and set the logs and tinder, ready to light. All was well then. Nurse was drinking a cup of tea, and Isabella was asleep.'

'And what time was it when she was discovered to be missing?'

'Isabella always has her breakfast at ten o'clock; but she did not ring, and the servants took it for granted that she was sleeping late because of—'

'Yes, yes, but what time was it?'

'Not until noon.'

'So there are six hours unaccounted for.' Cecily leant her forehead against her fingers, as two little furrows appeared between her brows. 'Did she dress herself? Has anyone checked to see if any of her clothes are missing?'

'She took nothing. It was the first thing I thought of.'

'And no one saw her leave the house?'

'She did not leave the house.'

'Whatever do you mean?'

'Ever since that terrible night when we found her in the crypt, her husband personally locks the door to her suite at night and keeps the key with him in his room. During the day, there is a footman outside the door.'

'I did not see him.'

'Nevertheless, he was there.'

'Perhaps he needed to—I mean, perhaps he left his post for a moment.'

'And just at that moment Isabella decides to escape?'

'Escape? That is a strange word to use.'

'It is how I see it. But it is of no consequence, because she did not escape.'

'And you say the house has been searched?'

'It has, from attics to cellars. We even sent two of the

footmen into the disused wing of the house where the timbers are all rotten. They found nothing.'

Cecily suddenly gave a start. 'Nurse! I had forgotten. Is she recovered?'

'She has a headache,' said Miss Proudie dryly. 'But she is not otherwise incommoded.'

Cecily looked up quickly. 'You don't like Nurse?'

'I do not think she has been especially helpful. I cannot see that her potions have done Isabella any good whatsoever. And, as a guardian, we see, she has been ineffectual.'

'She has only been here two days,' said Cecily, rather piqued. 'She is not a miracle worker.'

'No—just a witch,' said Miss Proudie, still in that dry tone. 'I have no patience with such wicked folly.'

'She does not claim to be! If the country people believe—it is hardly her fault.'

'Possibly. But the last thing Isabella needs is more superstitious nonsense talked about her.'

'Well, this is not helping,' said Cecily, rising from her chair. 'We must find her.'

'How?'

'We must use reason. If she did not leave her apartments by the door, she must have left by some other means. What of the windows?'

'Come up and see for yourself.' Miss Proudie led the way, as once before, through the narrow door. After about five minutes, they came to the tower suite, and now Cecily, on the lookout, saw the large, dependable looking footman seated in a shadowed alcove, watching the door. They entered.

All the windows in the three rooms, naturally enough, looked out of the tower across the park. They were small, no doubt for security in the days when the family would have sought refuge there from war or plague; and, although they opened inwards to admit fresh air, they were barred. Cecily conscientiously tested each bar. They were quite immovable.

'You see?' Miss Proudie could not keep a note of triumph

from her voice. 'We have already examined all that.'

'Very well. There must be a way out of the suite that is not generally known. The house is so old that there may be a hidden stair or passage. Perhaps a priest's hole?'

'Surely, her husband would have thought of it instantly if such a thing existed. It is inconceivable that he should have grown up here without knowing the secrets of the house.'

'His father died when he was very young. Perhaps it is one of those secrets that is passed on to the heir when he attains his majority and so has been lost.'

'I always deprecated your propensity for novel reading,' remarked Miss Proudie. 'However, I admit there seems no other explanation. I must learn from you how to search for a secret passage. I fear I have not read enough novels to have the least idea.'

'I have no notion either,' admitted Cecily. 'Perhaps we should examine the wainscot, one of those panels might slide open.' She thought for a moment. 'And I believe I have read about staircases hidden inside ancient chimney stacks.'

Miss Proudie was dubious, but she crossed to the fireplace and peered into the dark cavity. Fortunately, the fire had not yet been lit, as the household was too distressed to give any thought to customary tasks. Just then, a gust of wind came down the chimney, and a billow of sooty air sent Miss Proudie back into the room, coughing and spluttering, and with eyes watering.

'Oh, I am so sorry!' Cecily was distressed, although the fault was not hers. 'Do, please go, and wash that horrid stuff from your eyes. I shall be quite all right here with the footman outside.'

Miss Proudie, who was in some distress, needed no urging. She fairly ran from the room, so anxious was she to rinse the stinging soot from her face.

Seventeen: The Winding Stair

Cecily knew next to nothing about panelling, but even she could see that the oak wainscoting in the room was extremely ancient. There were few of the decorative flourishes of later centuries. It was very plain, and there were no sconces, brackets, or carvings to be pressed, turned or generally fiddled with. However, she conscientiously went about the room, knocking on the panels and listening for the hollow ring that would betray a concealed opening.

She was engaged in sounding the boards of a panel just above the skirting board when she straightened quickly, casting an uneasy glance around the chamber. She was quite alone, yet she felt that she was being watched. She gave herself a little mental shake and continued the work. But still she sensed eyes following her about the room. They were not friendly eyes.

Was this the feeling that had so terrorized poor Isabella? Out of the corner of her eye, she caught a sudden movement where no movement should have been. It seemed no more than a shifting in the light, but a cold terror seized her. She whirled around, but all was now still. She crossed the room. Could anyone be concealed in the shadows? Then she saw a mirror hanging on the wall above the dresser, and she laughed.

'Frightened of your own reflection, you poor fish?' How Dominic would have laughed. Then she thought, 'Why did I not notice the mirror before? I could have sworn it was a portrait hanging there.'

As she looked into the glass, she noted that there was a smudge of soot on her cheek and glanced down to take a handkerchief from her reticule. She tipped a little of the lavender water she carried onto the cambric and turned back to the mirror. Then she dropped both bottle and handkerchief to the floor, lifted her hand to her throat, and uttered a strangled scream. The face looking back at her was not her own!

Cecily staggered back, unable to tear her eyes from those

of the woman in the glass. She tripped upon the edge of a fine Aubusson rug and instinctively flung out a hand to save herself. Her hand knocked against the edge of the fireplace as she fell, and she cried out in pain. One leg was bent under her; the other skidded across the polished wood of the floor and hit the base of the wall. There was a horrid grinding noise of stone on stone and, then, as she watched, a narrow fissure appeared within the inglenook. She had found the hidden stair!

All this had taken but a split second. She turned her head to look back at the strange face and found to her utter amazement that there was no face—and no mirror. There was only a woman's portrait hanging on the wall—the portrait of the woman she had just seen in the mirror. But—had there been the faintest sound—as of something sliding into a groove—and the very softest click?

All at once, Cecily was not afraid any more. At night, upon wits already drugged into acceptance, she could imagine that such tricks might serve. But it was broad day, and she was in her right mind. She raised a sceptical eyebrow and addressed the portrait in a sarcastic tone. 'It is possible to over-egg the pudding, you know.' Then, firmly turning her back, she picked up a candle, lit it at the oil lamp, and held it to the gap in the inglenook.

It was surprisingly clean. She had expected cobwebs, mouse droppings and, perhaps, a few beetles; but the stairs looked freshly swept, and the air was sweet. Trying very hard not to think of what Dominic would say when he learned what she had been about, she stepped out of the room and onto the stair.

Then, realising that she was being very stupid indeed, she moved quickly out again. Seizing an embroidered footstool from in front of the fire, she wedged it securely in the fissure to prevent its closing behind her. But what if the villain entered the room, removed the stool, and shut her in? The itch to discover just what lay behind that picture was almost irresistible— She was still hesitating when Miss Proudie came back into the room.

She had washed away the soot and changed her gown and, as a result, appeared once more reassuringly normal. 'Goodness! You have found it!'

Cecily smiled modestly. She did not disclose that the discovery had been an accident, which was, she felt, irrelevant. 'Yes, and now you are here, I am going to explore. This must be the way Isabella left the room—or, as I think, was taken—'

'Be careful, dear Lady Cavendish!'

'I will. But listen Miss Proudie. You know that poor Isabella believes the first Lady Guisborough haunts her?' Miss Proudie nodded. 'Well, I think I know how the trick is worked. Pray stand in front of that picture and do not be alarmed at what you see.'

She stepped once more into the stairwell and, glancing to her left, immediately perceived a narrow passage that followed the outline of the inner wall. Within a few paces, she cracked her shin against something hard and, reaching down with the candle, she found she had knocked over a little joint stool. She set it upright, stood upon it, and discovered that four blocks of the original stone wall had been removed, forming an opening about two feet square. The opening was blocked by a square of canvas, which, she guessed, was the portrait. She set down her candle and then gasped in shock. Her hands were glowing. Then common sense reasserted itself. This was no more supernatural than the other. She lifted them to her nose and sniffed cautiously. Her fingers smelled of rotten eggs.

'Miss Proudie, can you hear me?' she called.

'Perfectly,' came the prompt reply.

'Is there not a substance—I cannot recall the name of it— that glows in the dark and gives off a noxious smell?'

Miss Proudie was far too intelligent to imagine this to be a non-sequitur. 'Phosphorus! You have found phosphorus?'

'It is all over my fingers.' She wiped her hand on her

skirts, leaving a trail of sickly light. Picking up the candle, she examined the back of the picture. There was a narrow, little shelf at the base. She pushed slightly, and the canvas obediently slid a little along the groove. Then, scanning either side of the canvas by the light of her candle, she quickly perceived a sheet of mirrored glass that ran in a second groove, parallel to the first. In this way, the mirror could be substituted for the canvas. But how could the exchange be effected without the occupant in the room being aware? It must be done in a split second at precisely the right time.

Once more, she lifted her candle and, standing on tiptoe, she found two little oval pieces of cardboard pinned to the canvas. She removed the pins and the cardboard. Good heavens! That was why she felt as though she were being watched. Through those little slits she could see Miss Proudie, staring into the picture as though entranced. 'Pray, Ma'am, turn your back for a moment, until I say you may look.'

Miss Proudie did as she was bid. Cecily slid the canvas to the side, and the mirror glided noiselessly into its place. She examined the back of the glass. It was silvered, as with any normal mirror; but there was an oval in the centre where the alloy had been scraped away, leaving only the faintest trace. Cecily pressed her face to this oval and called out, 'Turn around now, if you please, Ma'am.'

Miss Proudie turned, screamed, pressed her hand to her heart, and promptly fainted. Quite conscience stricken, Cecily jumped down from the stool and ran from the passage to the elderly lady's side. Fortunately, Miss Proudie's eyelids were already fluttering open. 'My—my—vinaigrette,' she murmured. Cecily opened the black satin reticule that hung from the lady's wrist and pulled out the smelling salts, which she held under Miss Proudie's thin nostrils.

'Oh, I do beg your pardon,' she exclaimed. 'I should have prepared you. But I wanted to know how convincing the illusion was.'

Miss Proudie managed a sour smile. 'I can attest—very

convincing.'

'And you could hear me quite well, too, could you not?'

'As though you were in the room.'

'So poor Isabella could have been worked on in that way, too. I mean, if a voice she thought to be Caroline's told her to get out of bed and follow her, don't you think she would probably obey?'

'In a drugged state? I should say, certainly.'

Cecily heaved a deep sigh of satisfaction. 'So, that is how it is done. All we need to know now is why. What possible benefit can anyone—anyone sane—derive from these horrid tricks?'

'Perhaps that is your answer. He is not sane.'

'You mean the Earl?'

'Who else?'

'Dominic doesn't believe it. He says Lord Guisborough is a very good fellow, and my husband, you know, is a judge of men. He has had to be.'

Miss Proudie snorted. 'Be that as it may—Isabella is still missing.'

'Very true—and I was just waiting for you to return before I explore the stairs. I think they lead to the roof, and that was where she was found once before, was it not?'

'It was one of the first places we searched,' objected Miss Proudie.

'Well, perhaps she was kept—secreted—in the passage until after the searchers had left.'

'Why on earth?'

'Oh, to make it all more mysterious and supernatural. I am beginning to understand how this murderer's mind works—whoever it is.' As she spoke, she lifted the candle and stepped through the narrow gap beside the fireplace. In a moment, she was ascending a winding stone stairway of obvious antiquity. The steps were narrow and so shallow that she had to proceed almost on tiptoe.

Before she had made more than a few turns, she heard a

sudden cry and a thud as of a body falling. The faint glow of daylight from the open fissure was blocked, as though someone was standing in the opening. Then, to her horror, she heard a step on the stairs below her. She blew out her candle and shrank back against the wall. There was not room for anyone to pass her without being aware of her presence. Oh, why had she not thought to provide herself with a weapon of some kind? Even a kitchen knife would have given her courage. Then, as she pressed her hands against the wall behind her with some idea of making herself as inconspicuous as possible, her right hand met with—not stone but empty air. She gave a stifled gasp. There was another passage off the stairs corresponding to the one below. She slipped gratefully into the darkness. There must be a network of these vantage points, she thought.

The footsteps grew closer. The tread was light and measured; she could hear low, even breathing. The figure was calmly making its way to the top of the staircase. Was it perhaps unaware that she had entered the hidden door? She tried to think who knew she was in the house. Surely, only the butler who had admitted her and, of course, Miss Proudie. Perhaps he thought it was Miss Proudie who had found that hidden door. No, it could not be so—someone had watched her from the mirror. But who? Then she saw a cloaked figure at the end of the little passage. It looked neither to the left nor right but proceeded calmly by the light of a dark-lantern, the beam of which shone only on the stairs. Then, for a moment, the lantern was lifted and, as Cecily shrank back, she caught a glimpse of a pink and white profile framed by golden ringlets, peeping from beneath the hood. Alana! It had been the doctor's sister all along!

Then she was gone, and Cecily almost sank to the floor as her knees gave way beneath her. She remained there for a few moments while she fought the faintness that threatened to overcome her. A few deep breaths soon revived her, and the dreadful sick feeling subsided. Now—what to do?

The sensible course would be, naturally, to retrace her steps and rejoin Miss Proudie, always assuming she could find the way to open the stone entrance from the inside. But what if Isabella did indeed lie helpless upon the roof. What might Alana do to her in the time it took Cecily to summon aid?

She began cautiously to move back along the passage to the stairs. There she paused to listen. The light footsteps had ceased. She heard a faint sound. It was very like the grinding sound she had heard when the opening had been revealed. A sudden draft of cold, fresh air lifted the ringlets at the back of her neck. She could not help congratulating herself on the soundness of her deductions. The stairway did, indeed, open onto the roof.

She put one foot on the stairs and then stopped with a sudden exclamation of annoyance. Below her was the sound of running feet, and Miss Proudie calling to her. 'Lady Cavendish—oh, Lady Cavendish. Where are you?'

'Shhh! She is here—on the roof,' she called softly, just as Dominic burst out of the shadows. Directly behind him, cursing fluently in French, came Raoul Saint Michel. Miss Proudie, pale and dishevelled, was at their heels and then the butler, very much out of breath. Cecily clutched at her husband. 'It is Alana! She is trapped—go and get her!'

Dominic thrust her to one side and took the stairs two at a time. She staggered; and Raoul, ever the gentleman, steadied her as he, in his turn, bounded past. Cecily, with a quick, apologetic, smile and a pat of the shoulder to Miss Proudie, followed them.

By the time she reached the roof, the chase was on. Alana leapt nimbly as a gazelle over every obstacle, dodging behind turrets and leaping over skylights, with as much ease as though she had been the spirit she impersonated. But she had already exerted herself too much that afternoon. Dominic gained steadily upon her. She swerved and headed back towards the doorway where Cecily stood watching. She flung aside her lantern, which fell to the leads with a crash and a tinkling of glass. The candle within guttered and died. She came on, fumbling beneath her cloak. Then, as the clouds lifted and a gleam of sunshine illuminated the soaked roof, Cecily saw that Alana held a dagger in her raised hand. As she gazed in horror, quite unable to move, the girl leapt at Dominic, her feet slid out from under her on the rain slick leads, and she fell sprawling with a shriek of maniacal rage.

In an instant, Dominic was beside her. He wrenched the dagger from her hand and flung it aside. Then, with an arrested expression, he stared down at the girl 'Well, well, well,' he said with a rather breathless laugh. 'What very unmaidenly behaviour, to be sure!'

Eighteen: Lady Cavendish Renounces Crime

They found Isabella, lying unconscious upon the leads at the very place from which her predecessor had jumped—or been thrown.

Dominic bent over her anxiously and laid two fingers to the side of her neck, feeling for a pulse. His eyes met Cecily's across the huddled form, and he smiled but did not speak because, at that moment, Isabella opened her eyes in a look of absolute terror. Cecily immediately seized one of her cold, clawed hands. 'There, there, my dear, there is nothing to be frightened of now. You are quite safe.'

'I saw her again—in daylight this time—and—she bade me—follow, but I could not. I think I fainted.'

'Very likely. But what you saw wasn't the first Lady Guisborough. It was just a wicked trick to frighten you,' interpolated Miss Proudie, who had finally emerged from the top of the winding stairs. 'Lady Cavendish found the secret of it and half scared me to death, too.'

'I am sorry for that Ma'am,' said Cecily, contritely. 'Presently, I shall show you how it was done, Isabella.'

She seemed scarcely to understand. 'How it was—done? What—?'

'Later, I think, Lady Cavendish. She needs to rest in the warm and be calm, now.'

Dominic, wasting no words, swooped down upon Isabella and picked her up in his arms. 'Just put your arms around my neck, and don't swoon off again. There is no need, I promise you.'

Within a very few minutes, Isabella was back in her bedchamber with Nurse, pale but composed, at her side. 'What you need, my Lady, is a nice cup of tea.' She bustled out to bring the boiling kettle from her own room.

Just then, they heard footsteps and voices outside the chamber. Lord Guisborough, with Mr Tweedie at his shoulder, ran headlong into the room. 'You found her! Thank God—oh, thank God!'

Ignoring everyone else in the room, he strode to his wife's side as she lay on the chaise longue, knelt beside her, and took her hand in his, kissing it passionately. 'My love, my little, little love!'

Isabella fixed her eyes on his face but withdrew her hand. 'No—*she* is watching—it angers her.'

Cecily started forward. 'But, Isabella—did you not hear? There is no ghost. It was all a wicked hoax—a plot! There is nothing more to be afraid of.'

Guisborough lifted his head and stared at her. 'You know this?'

'I shall show you.' She moved to the fireplace and, after a few moments, found the stone her hand had crashed against as she fell. She pressed the place, and the fissure appeared as noiselessly as before. 'Wait here,' she commanded, and slipped into the passage. A moment later, they could hear her voice behind the portrait. 'See how it slides away,' she said, demonstrating. 'And, then, the mirror takes its place.' She pressed her face against the glass. 'See, this is your ghost.'

Isabella sat up, pressing her palm to her forehead. 'But—but—oh, what a fool I have been. It would not deceive a child!'

'You were drugged, Isabella. In your right mind, no doubt you would have discovered the deception just as Lady Cavendish has done,' said Miss Proudie.

The Earl strode across the room to Cecily, his face alight. 'Lady Cavendish! How can I thank you Ma'am for what you have done? Your courage and resource have, I make no doubt, saved my poor wife's life.'

Cecily blushed and would have spoken, but the Earl continued, 'She still looks very poorly. We must have Stewart see to her. He will be glad to know that—'

'There is no need to send for the doctor, Guisborough,' said Dominic. 'He is already here.'

'Then pray ask him to attend us,' said the Earl.

Dominic stepped to the still open fissure and called up the

stairs. 'Hi! Raoul, beg the good doctor to join us!'

There was an odd stillness in the room as they listened to the sounds of feet upon the stairs, the muttered French imprecations, and almost animal sounds that greeted them. Then, quite suddenly, the figure of a woman was projected into the chamber at the toe of the Marquis' boot. It sprawled in front of the Earl, strange and ungainly in white draperies, the golden hair dishevelled, the incongruously muscular and hairy arms splayed at an odd angle. Its distorted face was smeared with rouge and powder which the rain had turned into a goblin mask.

'What the Deuce—?' the Earl began, then was silenced as the golden head was raised and mad, blue eyes gazed into his. 'Hector?'

The words that spewed from the doctor's mouth were mostly unfamiliar to Cecily, but she was hardly surprised when her husband strode towards him. 'Shut your mouth, you damned lunatic. There are ladies present—' As he caught the doctor by the scruff of the neck, the golden wig came away in his hand, and he flung it from him with an exclamation of disgust. He thrust the doctor back to the floor. 'Another word, and I'll shut it for you for good.'

At this moment of high drama, Nurse came in with a maidservant at her heels bearing a tray. Superbly ignoring the doctor sprawled upon the floor, she set it down. 'This will make you feel much better, my Lady,' she remarked as she lifted a pot of honey and prepared to sweeten the hot drink.

Cecily stared, oddly disturbed. Something in the back of her mind clicked—honey? Honey! Honey in Isabella's tea— honey on Alana's tea tray—honey in Michael Sullivan's hot milk—the unopened jar at the Manor— 'Don't! Don't give it to her!' she cried. 'Don't you see? It is the honey!'

Raoul, his quick French wits the first to understand, snatched the jar from Nurse's hand. 'Where did you get this,' he demanded of Isabella.

'Doctor Stewart,' she said in a bewildered tone. 'It is from his own beehives. It is—he said it is—very good for me. Because of the special nectar the bees feed upon.'

Mr Tweedie was ashen. 'Stewart? You have not—you did not give your patients honey from the moonflowers I gave you? I particularly warned you—'

'Moonflowers?' Raoul's voice came harsh and incisive. 'You don't mean *Datura*?'

'Yes—I—I brought some plants back from India, and Stewart took one from me. They have grown well. He has a fine border now. But I *told* him—'

'You told this *scélérat*—this assassin—that honey from bees that have fed upon the Datura plant will induce hallucinations, delirium, *l'amnésie*? But you are *un imbecile*!'

'But—but—why?' Isabella's voice was still weak, but the vagueness, the confusion, had dissipated. She sounded as though she really wanted to know. 'What have I ever done to deserve this of you?'

Doctor Stewart lifted himself from the floor and stood, arms folded, an incongruous but strangely menacing figure. He curled his lip and shrugged.

'Hector?' It was the Earl who spoke. 'For God's sake, man, explain yourself. I cannot believe you—you of all men—meant us harm.'

'Not you, Guisborough, only your wives,' interposed Dominic. 'I see it all now.'

Cecily exchanged a glance with her husband. 'Because of Alana?'

He nodded. 'He meant Alana to be the Countess of Guisborough, but you, my Lord, wouldn't co-operate. You liked Alana well enough but thought of her as a child still. And worse, you would keep falling in love and getting married.'

Cecily took up the tale. 'So your wives had to be removed. And, after the death of two wives in such dreadful circumstances, you would have found it hard to persuade anyone else to marry you. And the odds were that, eventually, you would have turned to Alana.'

'But Alana had other ideas,' said Dominic with a significant smile. 'She liked you, but young Repton won her heart, and so she, too, was drugged; and, under the influence of the drug—'

'She was persuaded to believe the Earl was—what was it she said—"the handsomest, most charming, kindest, and best man I have ever known." She said it in the oddest tone, too—as though she were reciting a lesson.'

'That is exactly what she was doing.'

'And then he set it about that she was mad, just so he could keep her confined and at his mercy. That was even more wicked than all the rest. Poor, poor girl.'

The Earl paced back and forth across the chamber, his restless energy and anger demanding an outlet. He stopped suddenly and barked out, 'All this so that his sister should be my wife? Why?'

'Money, my dear Sir. What else?'

'But—there would have been nothing beyond the usual marriage settlements, and those would have been arranged with her parents, not her brother. It cannot justify two murders—even to a madman.'

'I fancy, Guisborough, that you would not have long survived once your new Countess had produced an heir. As uncle and, almost certainly guardian, of the child, he might plunder the estate at will.'

'But what if there were no heir?'

'Oh, there would have been an heir. Who better placed than the family physician to ensure that there was a child, and a child of the right sex, too?'

'You mean—?'

'If Alana proved barren, or produced a girl, I fancy he would have arranged matters. Any cottager's child would do.'

Raoul nodded. 'It is true. The *bébé*, it makes its appearance in the warming pan, and who is to know?'

'Only the good doctor.'

'But what of Michael?' said Cecily. 'Why harm that dear little boy?'

Dominic looked with contempt at the doctor, who stood apparently divorced from the proceedings. 'Our doctor has a tidy mind. Michael was a loose end—he had to be cut off.'

'Such wickedness,' pronounced Miss Proudie. 'But "vengeance is mine, sayeth the Lord."'

'In this instance,' said Dominic with grim satisfaction, 'Vengeance is likely to come at the hands of the hangman— and a very good riddance.'

* * * * *

'It is quite amazing,' said Cecily, as the six friends were assembled in the drawing room at Maythorpe Manor, 'how any group of quite ordinary people can look so very suspicious. I could have believed any one of a dozen people to be the murderer.' She thought for a moment. 'Well, perhaps not quite a dozen, but you know what I mean.'

Kate nodded. 'That is because everybody has something to hide. They do not care if it obfuscates—is that the right word—the case.'

Lion slid an arm around her shoulders. 'What do you have to hide, my dearest girl?'

She leant back against his shoulder, smiling. 'Why, I should hate anyone to suspect that I am so odiously commonplace as to adore my own husband.'

Dominic, impatient of this discursion into sentiment, dragged the conversation back to the investigation. 'Old Tweedie was a bit of a false trail. I was convinced at one point that he was hiding something.'

'Oh, he was,' said Raoul with a grin. 'He and I shared a bottle or two one night last week, and he told me the whole. *Le vieux imbécile*—he was drummed out of the East India Company for cheating at faro. And why, you ask me, should he have cheated at cards? I will tell you. Because he badly needed money to provide for the Nautch girl and her little bastard he kept hidden away in the town. This so godly man broke every commandment except one—he did not kill.'

'Then you picked on that poor young man—what is his name? The apothecary's son,' Cecily reminded her husband.

Dominic shrugged. 'He was a possibility. He had lost his sweetheart; you could say he was temporarily off his head.'

'Well, he is quite all right now,' said Kate. 'Devoting himself to good works and helping my poor Lion around the parish.'

'And then, of course, Miss Proudie suspected poor little Marie-Claire. She is pretty and French, and that is enough to condemn her.

Dominic laughed. 'I understand she has left the household and is established under the protection of a lucky young officer in Lincoln.'

Raoul made a little grunt signifying approval, which earned him a stern look from his wife. 'Well, *ma belle*, every young man should—er—gain experience. And a Frenchwoman—as you know—'

'For all you know, she may make him an excellent wife,' said Cecily, rather primly. 'And I do not see what there is to laugh at!'

'No—no—do not eat me. It is as you say. All *I* say is that he will be a very lucky young man if she does consent to marry him. But I hear she is aiming higher than that. There is a young colonel in Lincoln who is also *très épris*— A pity, she improved the scenery.'

Cecily giggled a little. 'How very ungallant of you to suggest that there are no other pretty women in Alford.'

'Now you know I meant nothing of the kind,' he protested, throwing up his hands.

'There is Alana,' said Dominic in a more sober tone. 'What Stewart did to his sister was—'

'Evil,' said Cecily. 'Quite evil, that poor, poor girl.'

'After the night of the storm, I was convinced she was behind the whole thing.'

'I know. I am so glad she had nothing to do with it. I like her so much.'

'So she and young Repton will be married?' said Abby. 'They will make a pretty pair.'

'Yes, I shall call the banns next Sunday,' said Lion with satisfaction.

'I wonder if he knows she is five years older than him.'

'Dominic!'

'How do you know?' asked Abby.

'Her brother told me.'

'Well, it is not that he has ever lied before,' remarked Raoul.

Dominic grinned. 'If you think about it, she must be. Because he was hoping to marry her off to Guisborough before he married Caroline. Guisborough isn't the man to marry a child out of the schoolroom. And he was married to Caroline six years ago.'

'Oh. Well, we cannot worry about that. I daresay Mr Repton will not give a fig,' said Cecily.

'No, because there is no one to tell him,' said Dominic with a grin. 'I shall not.'

'Doesn't it have to go on the marriage certificate?' she asked rather anxiously.

'I shall turn a blind, clerical eye,' Lion assured her.

'Well, then that's all right.'

'And Guisborough is sending Michael to Switzerland, I hear. His illness was not all Stewart's doing then?' said Kate.

'Well, his damnable honey did nothing to help the poor little fellow, but the underlying disease is real enough. They do not think he is consumptive, however. With cleaner air, he should soon grow strong again.'

'Another murderer disposed of,' said Dominic, holding out a hand to his wife. 'And it is all because of you, my darling.'

She took his hand and carried it to her cheek. 'Not really, you know. In fact I was very stupid. The doctor himself practically told me the truth during our first meeting, but I did not see it.' She saw that they were all staring at her and dimpled. 'You see we were talking about ghosts and legends and he told me, quite openly, that an ancestor of his had gone mad and murdered his wife and children—with an axe.'

'He actually told you there was madness in the family?' said Dominic in a faint voice. 'And you never thought to mention it?'

She gave a little shrug. 'Sorry.'

'Well,' said Abby, 'I still think you were excessively clever to find the secret stairway.'

Cecily giggled. 'Actually, that was an accident. I fell and my hand hit the right stone be accident.'

Lion smiled. 'The thing is, Cecily, no one else has these accidents. I fear you will have to accept the credit for solving this mystery whether deserved or no.'

'Yes, but this will have to be my last case—at least for a little while.' She turned shining eyes upon her husband. 'And I am afraid, dearest, that I shall not be able to accompany you to Africa in the spring, after all. Because, you see I shall be— otherwise engaged.'

The three men looked rather bewildered, but Abby jumped up from her seat and flew to embrace her. 'Oh, Cecily, how lovely! When is it to be?'

'In March, so Nurse says.'

'What—? Dominic rose from his seat, a dazed look in his eyes.

'Oh, do not be such a goose, Dom. You are going to be a father!' cried Abby.

Dominic knelt beside his wife's chair and took her in his arms. 'Darling, is this true?'

Cecily patted his cheek in a very maternal way and said, 'Certainly it is true. And that is why I am obliged to renounce all interest in crime—for now.

The End

CPSIA information can be obtained
at www.ICGtesting.com
Printed in the USA
LVHW081200291118
598641LV00014B/426/P